THE CLASSROOM

Student Council Smackdown!

THE CLASSROOM

Student Council Smackdown!

Directed by Robin Mellom

Filmed by Stephen Gilpin

Disney • Hyperion Books
New York

For Luke
—R.M.

For Makena as she departs middle school.
I hope it was fun.
—S.G.

Text copyright © 2013 by Robin Mellom
Illustrations copyright © 2013 by Stephen Gilpin

Printed in the United States
First Edition
1 3 5 7 9 10 8 6 4 2

V567-9638-5-12105

Library of Congress Cataloging-in-Publication Data

Mellom, Robin.
  The classroom: Student council smackdown! / by Robin Mellom; art by Stephen Gilpin.—1st ed.
      p. cm.
  Summary: Chronicles the race for seventh grade class president at Westside Middle School as suddenly popular documentary-film subject Trevor Jones faces his best friend, Libby Gardner, and Cindy Applegate, the official school gossip.
  ISBN 978-1-4231-5064-0 (alk. paper)
  [1. Middle schools—Fiction. 2. Schools—Fiction.
3. Popularity—Fiction. 4. Elections—Fiction. 5. Politics, Practical—Fiction. 6. Best friends—Fiction. 7. Friendship—Fiction.
8. Documentary films—Production and direction—Fiction.] I. Gilpin, Stephen, ill. II. Title.
  PZ7.M16254Cls 2013
  [Fic]—dc23   2012040446

Reinforced binding

Visit www.disneyhyperionbooks.com

SUSTAINABLE FORESTRY INITIATIVE   Certified Sourcing
www.sfiprogram.org
SFI-00993

THIS LABEL APPLIES TO TEXT STOCK

WESTSIDE
MIDDLE SCHOOL

DAY
18

>>Production: THE CLASSROOM

Over on Miller Street, behind the brick walls of Westside Middle School, there are desks. There are lockers. There are worksheets, textbooks, pencils, pens, and squeaky hallway floors that are buffed clean every Friday, right around four.

But really, it's more often four thirty or four forty-five, since Wilson, the janitor who shall not be called a janitor, is a very busy man.

At Westside Middle School you will find teachers, a principal, counselors, and, of course, students. One of those students is Trevor Jones—your normal, average, everyday, slightly neurotic, often embarrassed, usually-slipping-on-something, (but this one time) totally epic student.

This documentary set out to tell the story of Trevor and his also-sometimes-epic-but-usually-normal classmates. It was our hope to reveal the brighter side of middle school. But from what we uncovered, things have gotten pretty dark for the kids at Westside. You are about to witness several moments of the not-so-bright side of Westside Middle School.

And somehow Trevor Jones ends up in a hairnet. So awkward.

However, this documentary will also reveal how Trevor and his friends managed to turn things around.

Westside is their middle school.

And these are their stories.

Libby Gardner

7th grader
Waiting for the bus,
looking nervous

7:51 a.m.

I have to talk to Trevor about what happened over the weekend. But I'm not sure I'm ready to.

Everything was fine when I saw him on Friday. I was working on my campaign posters, and he was talking about how he was picked second for a volleyball team in P.E., which is MONUMENTALLY huge, and we were both excited and— Oh, wait! I haven't explained about the posters yet.

See, I'm running for class president, which I've done every year since fourth grade, and I hired Trevor as my campaign manager, also another thing I've done every year since fourth grade. I guess I like tradition. Anyway, everything was going according to plan until Sunday. When I got the news.

I was talking to my cousin Luke, who's in tenth grade. And here's the thing: he told me the truth about middle school. The whole ENTIRE truth.

After carefully reviewing all the information

he provided me, I reached one simple conclusion: everything I thought I knew about how to run for office is just . . . wrong. So pretty much, my dreams of presidency are in the trash. No joke, I threw away all my posters. So now I have nothing . . . no plan, no ideas. I'm a blank slate of nothingness.

[lets out a long sigh]

And the thing is, Luke didn't stop at just advice on my campaign. We talked about Trevor, too.

Trevor's not going to want to hear what I'm about to tell him.

[clutches her stomach]

I feel a little pale.

CHAPTER ONE

WHEN ASKED HOW THEY KNEW **TREVOR JONES,** most kids would say it was because of the fall dance. The one where Trevor drenched Corey Long with orange soda and sent him running into the girls' bathroom.

Since Corey Long had harassed many kids at some point over the years, the Orange Soda Incident of Several Days Ago was quite agreeable to most.

However, there were a few kids who would say they knew the name Trevor Jones because he was the one who had fought Corey Long with nunchucks in a heated battle in a darkened alley. And there were two guys who claimed to know the name Trevor Jones because he was the one who hacked into the FBI computer mainframe.

The gossip flew fast at Westside Middle School. And the gossip was often inaccurate.

Nonetheless, Trevor Jones was now experiencing high levels of popularity, or at least *way* higher than he'd ever experienced before. It was as if an invisible barrier had been lifted, and Trevor was now experiencing life in a dimension he never knew existed.

In the several days since the dance, he'd received head nods and high fives from people—some of whom he didn't even know—as he walked down the hall. At lunch, groups of kids (cool ones!) would scoot over to make room for him. They'd ask him questions. Nod. Smile. All that. Sometimes he'd even have a choice of different groups to sit with because they each wanted him to join theirs.

But truth be told, what Trevor was enjoying *most* about his newfound popularity? P.E.

The part where they picked teams. Trevor was now getting picked nearly at the beginning, rather than having to pace the blacktop or gym floor or soccer field until the very end, wondering if he'd *ever* get picked.

For Trevor Jones, life in middle school had suddenly taken a turn for the awesome.

FOUND IN TREVOR'S NOTEBOOK

Even though Libby certainly missed hanging out with Trevor at lunch, she didn't mind Trevor's newfound popularity one bit. Trevor being socially active meant she was that much closer to retirement as his personal social director. Libby had been quite busy in the days since the dance. She'd been feverishly preparing her campaign posters for the upcoming student class presidential election, which she'd been working on since the summer. Being prepared was Libby's favorite way to approach things. Really, her only way.

The process of running for office was much different in middle school than in years past. In elementary school, the students just volunteered to give a fun one-minute speech during rainy-day recess, and the kids voted with "heads down, eyes closed!"

In middle school elections, they were required to complete an "intent to run" application, write an essay, and get four teachers to sign off in support of their nomination.

But even though the election process was intense, Libby Gardner, as always, was prepared.

Or so she thought.

On Monday morning, Trevor met Libby at the top of the street for the bus, as usual. As he approached her, a few guys waiting around for the bus nodded at him and said "Whassup," and one girl from down the street waved at him. Marty, his large eighth grade friend, who was wearing camouflage pants and a matching sweatshirt, also gave him a thumbs-up. It was the start of yet another good day.

Trevor tapped Libby on the shoulder. "I stapled those papers like you asked," he said.

But when she turned and looked at him, something was different. Her face. It was discolored. Pretty pale, as if she'd just witnessed something illegal. Or really un-alphabetized.

Trevor felt a slight shiver inside—it was an unshake-able sense that Libby needed to tell him something. He clutched the strap on his backpack. "Are you okay, Lib? What happened?"

But she stared straight ahead, not saying anything.

"Did your mom hit a raccoon with her car again?" Trevor was fully aware of Libby's affection for animals, particularly raccoons. It was their markings; just so cute.

"No," she whispered.

He leaned in closer since she clearly didn't want to share whatever this was with the rest of the kids standing at the bus stop. "The rabbits? They get to your romaine lettuce garden again?"

Libby took pride in the six varieties of romaine lettuce she grew—the red heirloom being the tastiest—and last year when the rabbits wiped them all out, she didn't speak for two whole days. Libby's goodwill toward animals did not extend to rabbits.

"It's not those stupid rabbits."

Trevor was relieved she was talking, at least.

"It's . . . it's . . ." She didn't have time to finish her sentence because the school bus lurched in front of them and pulled to a stop.

With her arms hanging at her sides, Libby said in a low voice, "I'll explain on the bus."

"Is it bad news?"

She turned to him, still looking like a ghost, but ignored the question and just climbed on.

Weird. That was weird. Trevor didn't get it—when he'd last seen Libby on Friday, she was happily shading accent colors on her election posters while he told her all about the awesomeness of being Brian Baker's second pick for his volleyball team in P.E.

And now *this*? The pale face of doom?

A pep talk, he thought. She probably just needs a pep talk about how green was the perfect color to choose for an accent on her campaign poster.

But just before he stepped onto the bus, Marty grabbed him by the shoulder. "Dude, something's wrong with Libby. I've seen that face on my older sister."

"You have?"

"It's the something-happened-over-the-weekend face."

"I figured that."

Marty clamped down on his shoulder hard. "Listen, dude. These are *girls* we're talking about. Go in cautiously. Let her talk first. Give her space. Don't ask too many questions . . . but ask just enough."

"Right. Not too many questions, but enough of them. I get it."

Trevor didn't get it. He needed a number. Two? Four? How many questions were *too* many? But before he could ask Marty, Trevor looked around and realized he was the only one left standing on the curb. Quickly, he jumped onto the bus and smoothly high-fived several kids as he made his way down the aisle—which made him feel pretty rad—then slid into the seat next to Libby. And he had no idea what to ask.

For three blocks they rode in silence. She wasn't explaining herself. Not a word. By the fourth silent block, he looked over at her and then wished he hadn't. The look on her face, the lack of color, the silence—it was all so unlike her. Had someone kidnapped his best friend and replaced her with an alien?

Time to get to the truth. "Libby, just tell me. You don't like the way I stapled your campaign papers. Is that it?"

Libby decided she'd have to tell him about this past weekend—about how everything she thought she knew about elections and popularity and poster making had come to a screeching halt.

Over the summer, not only had she been working on her campaign for student class president, but she'd been gathering all the information she could about middle school. She'd done research online, watched hour after hour of tween television shows set in middle schools, and most important, she'd interviewed real people who had made it through middle school—*survivors*.

It turned out some of her own family members were invaluable resources for middle school survival. Her seventeen-year-old cousin Lana from Flagstaff, for example, was very helpful in answering all things related to middle school dances.

Jenny, her second cousin on her dad's side, from Los Angeles, knew all about comfortable yet stylish footwear.

And her aunt Shelli in Atlanta gave her great advice on where to get school supplies at discount prices. Ninety-nine-cent file folders at Safe Mart!

But the one relative Libby wanted to talk to most was her fifteen-year-old cousin Luke in Sacramento. He'd actually attended Westside and had been elected president of his class two years in a row. Even as the new kid at his high school in Sacramento, he'd come close to winning freshman class president and was almost a definite to win as a sophomore. So Libby could hardly wait to discuss middle school elections with him—she had a long list of questions.

Still, Luke was a pretty popular guy. He was the lead

guitarist in his band, which often met for practice in his parents' garage. Luke and his band had even spent a few weeks at Rock Band Summer Camp because they took their craft seriously. But since he was so busy, Libby wasn't able to get hold of him until that Sunday. Finally they connected, and Luke agreed to video chat with her about elections as well as the other topic he knew *very* well: popularity.

Because if anyone understood popularity at Westside Middle School, it was Luke.

FROM THE ARCHIVES: WESTSIDE YEARBOOK

Jessica Galligan
Best Voice

Luke Gardner
More Popular than
EVERYONE

Ryan Garton
Most Organized

During their talk, Libby asked about debate preparation, and Luke talked about Rock Band Summer Camp. She asked about slogan ideas, and he talked about his new guitar. She was growing really anxious to get to campaign talk. At long last, Luke agreed to look at her campaign posters, but he took one glance and laughed. "Your motto is 'Get involved'?"

"Sure. Shouldn't I try to get the student body more involved in school activities?"

Luke really laughed at this, a full-on belly laugh. Libby was devastated—how could he be so rude? But when he finally pulled himself together, he explained to her exactly *how* to win a middle school student election.

But it was advice she wasn't expecting to hear.

As Libby sat on the bus next to Trevor, she wondered if it was a good time to tell him everything Luke had told her. Trevor had really been enjoying school with all his new-found popularity. But Trevor was now glaring at her as if he wanted an explanation, and she couldn't bear him not knowing the truth about her pale complexion. The entire truth.

She turned in her seat to face him. "I did some research. I didn't want to have to tell you this, but you need to know." She took a deep breath and let it out. "I video chatted on the Internet with my cousin Luke over the weekend."

"You use the Internet all the time, Libby. So why have you lost all the color in your face?"

"Because THIS time it was with *Luke*."

"Your cousin. The one in high school now?"

"Yeah. Tenth grade."

"The one who plays electric guitar all day?"

"Right."

Trevor smirked. "The same cousin who used to eat dirt when we were kids?"

"He doesn't do that anymore. Like I said, he plays guitar. And he also knows a lot about getting through middle school. You don't get to be the lead singer of a band like H2D without becoming popular."

"H2D?"

"Hostage to Democracy . . . I think. Or maybe it's Destruction—"

"Or Dirt."

Libby shrugged. "I can't remember. Anyway, he was the most popular kid at Westside when he was here. And he said the only way to win the election is to have a cool campaign. Apparently in middle school it's not just about ideas, it's mostly about the coolness of the presentation. Cool posters. Cool slogan. Cool *everything*."

Trevor nodded, unsure what the problem was. "Okay."

She poked him. "Me. Cool?"

"Sure."

"Do you have a fever, Trevor?"

"What do you mean? You're cool, Lib."

"No. *You're* the one who's cool now. *I'm* the one who rambles on and on about event planning and how important it is to implement good time management and—"

Trevor held his hand up. Excessive chatter meant she was getting nervous, and he needed to calm her down. "Let's just talk about your posters. At least you have those—"

"Yeah, see . . ." Libby bit at her lip. "Luke laughed at them. At first I just thought he was being rude. But then he started talking about all the elections he's won—some of them landslides. And after a while, I realized he was right. So I threw them away. They'll never work. The election is four days away and now I have nothing." She gripped the fabric at the hem of her skirt tightly. "My biggest dream is to be student class president, but it's feeling hopeless. How can I possibly pull something cool enough together?"

Trevor couldn't believe that after months of hard work, Libby would just throw away her posters because of one comment from her cousin. She was stronger than that. This wasn't like her. But if she wanted to start over from scratch only four days before the election, he'd find a way to help her out. "I'm your manager, Lib. I'll help you think up something."

Libby was appreciative of his help, and it was clear she needed to tell Trevor everything about that conversation with Cousin Luke, especially since the last part was about him. "Okay, so . . . about the 'cool' thing?" She winced. "There's more." She didn't want to have to tell Trevor this next part, but she felt she had to. She looked straight ahead as she said it, figuring the lack of eye contact would soften the blow. "Apparently, you can't do just one cool thing and expect it to last. You *always* have to do cool stuff. If you don't, popularity fades like one of those rub-on tattoos you get at the carnival. And if you make even one mistake—*poof!*—your popularity vanishes." She took a deep breath and delivered the final part of the news. "And apparently this last point was important because he leaned in close to the computer screen. He said guys like Corey Long *never* forget—they always get revenge."

Trevor swallowed hard. *ONE mistake is all it takes for me to lose my popularity? Corey Long is going to get revenge? Is there any other good news today?*

Libby looked over at him. "Oh, yeah, Luke also mentioned something about the importance of using deodorant, but then our Internet connection broke up. And I think that's it." She glanced down at her notes to make sure.

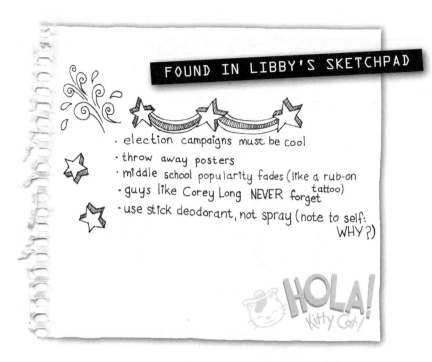

- election campaigns must be cool
- throw away posters
- middle school popularity fades (like a rub-on tattoo)
- guys like Corey Long NEVER forget
- use stick deodorant, not spray (note to self: WHY?)

HOLA! Kitty Cat!

Trevor wasn't sure what to think of all of this. True, Luke had grown up to be a cool guy, but there *were* those dirt-eating days. Could he be believed? And what was so important to know about deodorant? There *wasn't* anything, that's what.

"I can handle this, Libby. I can be cool all the time. Lots of people do it. Surely it's not that hard."

But truthfully, it was starting to sound hard to Trevor. His seemingly normal Monday had gone from high fives and awesomeness to bad news and sweaty palms.

To make matters worse, their bus had now pulled up to the curb at Westside, and Trevor could see groups of kids hanging around outside. And one of them was staring right at him.

Corey Long.

With his eyes narrowed, Corey gave him one of his trademark smirks—the intimidation smirk.

Instantly, Trevor's palms went a thousand times more clammy, and a bead of sweat formed on his temple.

Libby noticed Trevor and Corey staring each other down through the dusty bus window, sort of resembling angry cats in neighboring yards. The atmosphere was prickly.

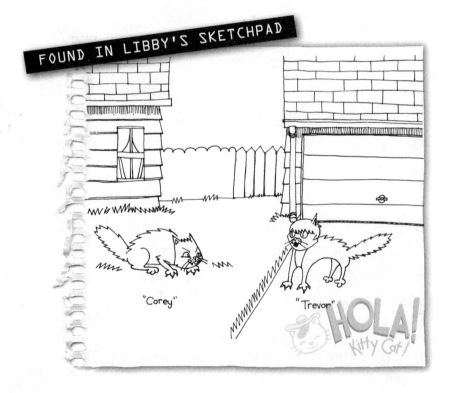

FOUND IN LIBBY'S SKETCHPAD

"Corey"

"Trevor"

HOLA! Kitty Cat!

"Told you." Libby dabbed at Trevor's sweat bead with a tissue. "But we have to go—class starts soon." She gathered her things and headed down the bus aisle ahead of him.

Trevor grabbed his backpack, and when he looked up, he saw some guys in the seats in front of him with their hands raised in ready position to give him a high five. Which normally would be a pretty awesome thing. But now with all this talk about being popular and *staying* popular, Trevor Jones was suddenly drowning in doubt.

One mistake, he thought. That's all it takes. And if there's anyone who can make one mistake and completely ruin his reputation . . . it's me.

Trevor Jones

7th grader
Sitting at the
back of the bus

8:15 a.m.

I don't get it. I'd been high-fiving and head-nodding people all last week just fine, no problem. And then Libby tells me this news about making ONE mistake and wham! Sweaty palms. Now I can't stop worrying.

I mean, what if I've been doing them wrong? The high fives. Like, am I supposed to have a flat palm? Or a slightly cupped palm to act like I care but not really? And should my fingers be split? Or tightly pulled together?

And don't even get me started on the head nods. Quick? Slow? Do I smile? Smirk? What?!

[takes a deep breath]

I'm exhausted.

Marty Nelson

8th grader

At the entrance of
Westside, holding
a magazine

8:16 a.m.

Sure, I've seen this before. A not-so-popular kid does something cool, gets popular, and then has to figure out a way to HANDLE it and gets freaked out. Happens all the time.

See, whenever I'M in a situation like that—when I'm worried about how to be popular and what to do and what to say—I just turn to page sixty-four in *Boys' Life* magazine.

[flips open magazine and points to article]

Right here. "Pike Fishing in Alaska." I just read this, because really . . . WHO CARES. Reading this is way more interesting.

Some good photos in here too. Check out the teeth on this northern pike!

CHAPTER TWO

LIBBY HAD ALREADY GONE AHEAD WITHOUT HIM, SO Trevor realized he would have to get off the bus, sneak past Corey, hurry down the hall, and make it to homeroom on time all on his own. And all without making one single mistake. He really just wanted to find a way to skip this day altogether. There are some days that should be avoided completely, and Trevor could tell this was going to be one of them.

"Off the bus, kid!" the driver yelled back at him.

Trevor looked up and realized all this worrying about getting off the bus had caused him to be the only one left on the bus. Even the kids who'd been waiting to give him high fives were gone.

Suddenly it felt as if he were at the base of Mount

M.t.Everest

Things I need:
climbing stuff
map
pants

Things I have:

tennis racket
baseball
backpack
three colors of ballpoint pens
highlighter (yellow)
deck of cards
yo-yo

Not really prepared for this.

Everest without any climbing gear or a map or even pants.

"Sorry, sir!" Trevor picked up his backpack and scampered off the bus.

Trevor made it into the school without incident and immediately started to scan the crowds to locate Corey Long. He needed to stay away from Corey's foot, as there was a high probability of it tripping him. And he also wanted to stay away from Corey's smirk due to the probability of it intimidating him.

Popping up on his tiptoes, Trevor searched for Corey's

head, with all its perfectly aligned hairs, but all he saw were buzz cuts, ponytails, and floppy messes. No Corey.

This was either good news or very bad news. Good in that perhaps Corey had grown bored waiting for Trevor and had gone to class or maybe even had gone on with the rest of his life.

A possibility, Trevor hoped.

Or bad news in that Corey was biding his time before exacting his revenge and would pop up in an unexpected time and place.

More than likely, Trevor warned himself.

As he turned the corner to head to homeroom in Mr. Everett's class, Trevor noticed a large group of seventh

"Corey Getting Revenge"

Oh, come on. During Thanksgiving dinner?
Really?

FOUND IN TREVOR'S NOTEBOOK

grade boys headed his way. They were smiling and had their hands raised, ready for high fives. Trevor's palms instantly went clammy. He quickly rubbed them dry on his jeans as a zillion thoughts went through his head about finger position. *Closed? Split?*

Time had run out—the guys were right there in front of him. Trevor went ahead and high-fived them as they walked past, not at all sure if his finger position was correct. No one seemed to notice, though, and Trevor felt a bit of relief . . . until the very last guy. His hand wasn't raised, and Trevor was left hanging. The kid wasn't smiling, either. Which wasn't a good thing considering this was Jake Jacobs, pretty much the most popular guy in seventh grade.

Jake was a skateboard fanatic and spent every after-school daylight hour at the skate park. He had long shaggy hair and only wore clothes designed by famous skateboarders. Jake was committed to the sport. And he was cool. It should be noted this was also the same guy Trevor once accidentally referred to as a girl due to Jake's confusing long hair.

Trevor assumed that Jake was now staring him down—not high-fiving him and not smiling—because he had not gotten over that incident. The moment had been cringe-worthy. Which was exactly what Trevor did now: cringed.

But then suddenly, Jake Jacobs lifted his hand—not for a high five but for the elusive fist bump. In the hierarchy of social greetings, those were rare and not to be taken lightly. "You're impressive, bro," Jake said.

Trevor made a fist and stared down at it for longer than a comfortable amount of time, trying to determine the best angle at which to match Jake's fist bump. He considered straight on. Then sideways. But ultimately Trevor just bumped Jake's in a rather awkward diagonal motion. But at least it was a bump. "Me? Impressive? Why?" Trevor asked.

Jake threw his hands in the air. "Dude, I can't believe you have the guts to high-five all these guys right *in front* of Corey Long!"

Trevor shuddered. Right in front . . . What?! He snapped his head up, and sure enough, several feet down the hall was Corey Long, leaning against the wall, watching him. He'd seen the entire thing.

Gulp.

"But I . . . I . . ." Trevor wanted to explain that he didn't intentionally do it and that he really, *really* could use an escort right about now.

"Corey knows you're popular because of what you did to him at the dance. You have no fear! No one *ever* stands up to that guy!" Jake continued, fully impressed with Trevor.

He leaned over and bumped shoulders. "Come sit with us at lunch today, bro."

As Jake and the guys walked on, Trevor locked eyes with Corey. Half of him felt sick with worry that all Corey had to do was take five measly steps forward and pummel him right then and there.

But the other half of him felt sick with excitement. Jake Jacobs had just invited him to eat lunch with him. That sort of thing didn't just happen! Jake was one of the most popular kids in his class, and even though a bunch of kids had been asking Trevor to eat with them at lunch, it had never occurred to him that he'd ever be invited by *Jake's* group. Breaking into that level of popularity had seemed impossible at this point in his life. Maybe if their moms had been best friends and a friendship had been forced between them—then sharing a lunch table would make sense. But becoming friends with Jake in seventh grade out of the blue? Unheard of! And all it took was high-fiving some guys in front of Corey Long?

This popularity thing is so easy, Trevor thought.

And yet also pretty complicated. Because now he had to figure out how to get past Corey without getting mangled so that he could make it to lunch with Jake and his friends.

Luckily, someone grabbed his elbow. "Oh-ma-god! Trevor! We have to get going if we're going to make it to homeroom on time!" Cindy Applegate, the official school gossip, led him down the hall, serving as a buffer between him and Corey.

He never thought he'd be this happy to see Cindy. The two of them walked down the hall together, and Trevor slinked right past Corey, keeping his eyes straight ahead. Within moments, he glanced back and saw that Corey had disappeared. Trevor had escaped getting pummeled, and for the first time—perhaps *ever*—was utterly relieved to be walking side-by-side down the hall with Cindy Applegate.

"Okay, so I *have* to talk to Libby," she said.

"What do you need to talk to Libby about?" he asked as he motioned her to the side. The halls were still bustling with kids rushing to get to class on time, so Trevor stepped out of traffic. Normally all this heavy activity made Trevor nervous, but right now he was just relieved to be rid of Corey. So far, even though this day was proving to be difficult, he was making it through just fine. Except—he had to be honest with himself—it was only 8:20 a.m.

"The election. I was hoping she'd give me the scoop about her campaign." Cindy popped in not just one piece of Hubba Bubba Strawberry Watermelon, but two. She often doubled up on gum during campaign season.

"You're running again?" he asked.

"Of course I am!"

Cindy had run against Libby every year since fourth grade. Even though there had been a pattern forming (Cindy won in fourth grade, Libby won fifth, Cindy won sixth), which meant Libby technically should win seventh grade, Cindy had decided that patterns were only good for locker wallpaper decoration. Truth be told, Cindy's locker decoration included much more than patterned wallpaper.

She scrunched her curls to make them curlier. "So, are you going to be Libby's manager again, or what?"

Trevor nodded. "Of course. Like every year." Then he cut his eyes back at her. "So who's going to be *your* manager?"

She dropped her chin to her chest. "I don't have one."

Trevor realized that maybe Cindy was struggling with her campaign, too. He couldn't help but feel a little relieved. Except that's when Cindy started bouncing. Really bouncing. "No, see . . . I didn't hire a manager—I hired a *team*! Team Cindy! Check it out!"

She hopped across the hall to her locker, where, sure enough, Team Cindy! was waiting for her.

Oh, no, Trevor thought. Cindy Applegate *is* going to have a cool campaign. With pom-poms and pep and exclamation points and everything. Libby doesn't have a chance.

Cindy Applegate

7th grader

Outside of homeroom, sprinkling glitter on her campaign brochures

8:25 a.m.

I should find out what kind of campaign Libby's planning. That girl's so organized, she's probably had it figured out for months.

I'm sure she did research, just like I did, and found out that student class elections are different from those in elementary school. In middle school it's a WHOLE different ball of wax paper.

Wait. That didn't make sense. Let me try that again.

We're in the big leagues now. We can't run for class president with just a few good ideas and a peppy speech. Nope, everything's different now. The campaign has to be cool. Slick. Flashy. You know . . . GLITTERY. Well, if that's what it takes to win, I'm on it! Finding uses for glitter is my favorite sport!

Okay, and also? Marty begged to be my campaign manager, which was sweet and all. But I'd already

35

hired Team Cindy! and there was NO WAY he'd fit into one of those T-shirts—we got a discount if we ordered them all the same size. And then I had to go ahead and tell him I didn't want to be boyfriend/girlfriend anymore. "Keeping my options open" is what they call it.

But honestly, I think I can win this thing with Team Cindy! We have a plan. And pep. And LOTS of T-shirts.

But I may need more glitter.

CHAPTER THREE

GATHERING HIS NERVE, **T**REVOR DECIDED THE BEST approach would be to rush up to Libby before homeroom began and tell her that Cindy had a cool campaign planned. Arming her with knowledge was the best thing he could do as her manager. Certainly he shouldn't let her be ambushed by Cindy with all her talk of pom-poms and matching T-shirts. It would send her into a spiral of doubt for sure.

As he entered the room, Trevor noticed his homeroom teacher, Mr. Everett, was busy untangling his solar system mobile. Perfect timing. Libby was headed to her seat in the front of the room, which was right next to Cindy, so that meant he had to put his plan into action—quick.

"Lib! Hold on a sec!" Trevor whisper-yelled to her.

Libby twirled around. "What is it? Class is about to start."

"It's about the election . . . there's something you need to know. Cindy is—"

But at that moment the bell rang, just as Mr. Everett untangled Mercury from Venus and called out triumphantly, "Everyone get seated. Class has started!"

Slinking back to his seat in the last row, Trevor looked away. He simply couldn't bear to watch the conversation that was about to happen between Cindy and Libby. No doubt Cindy would find a way to tell Libby all about her campaign plans even with Mr. Everett just three feet away. And watching Libby admit to Cindy that she had no election campaign planned out was something Trevor did not want to witness. Oh, the paleness.

Trevor slid into his seat and turned to his right; sitting next to him was Molly Decker. She was wearing black-and-white-striped tights and dark boots, and her blue highlights seemed to have gotten thicker over the weekend.

Molly often did her own highlight touch-ups—she felt changes were best if they weren't noticed. And since she didn't usually run into her classmates on the weekend, that meant it was the best time to make personal changes. No one ever seemed to pay attention.

"Nice highlights, Molly."

Except for Trevor. He always seemed to notice her subtle weekend changes.

She shrugged. "I went with Chunky Cobalt Number Seven this time."

"Good choice," he said, then turned to listen to the teacher.

Mr. Everett took roll, instructed the class to listen to the announcements, and then explained the procedure for storm safety. Trevor sweated through it all. There was just too much going on—how was he supposed to focus on his social life, Libby's election, *and* hurricane preparedness?

For the final few minutes of homeroom, Mr. Everett told the class to read while he graded papers. Trevor stared at the words in his copy of *Where the Red Fern Grows*, but he couldn't concentrate.

"What are you so worried about?" Molly blurted out to him.

He wiped his brow with the back of his hand. "Me? Worried? Nah. I'm fine."

"You keep looking over at Libby. You're sweating. And your book is upside down."

It was no use. He could never keep the truth from Molly—she'd been to multiple schools and had developed a keen sense for sniffing out drama. If someone were hiding the juicy tidbits of what was really going on, she'd demand the truth from them.

Or maybe it was just that he wanted to talk to someone and she was asking.

"It's Libby," he said. "She's running for class president, but she found out from her cousin Luke that her campaign needs to be cool."

Molly shrugged. "So?"

"So Libby's been working on a *very practical* campaign for months, so she threw away her posters and now she has to start over from scratch."

"So?"

"So Cindy is running against her and she *does* have a cool campaign with T-shirts and pom-poms and pep."

"So?"

"Didn't you hear me? I said *pom-poms*." He rubbed hard at the back of his neck. Did she not understand the gravity of the situation?

She picked a cuticle. "So . . ."

"So?! Stop saying 'so'! It means Libby's going to freak out when Cindy tells her that she has an amazing campaign already planned out. And Libby's going to be so embarrassed when she has to admit she has nothing planned with only four days to go before the debate. She'll be devastated."

"Trevor, if I could think of a word other than 'so' I would. But I can't."

"You don't think it's a big deal?"

Molly fiddled with the safety pin on her jacket, like this was starting to bore her. "She'll deal with it. It'll force her to come up with a plan to fix it."

Trevor looked over at Libby, who was straightening and restraightening her skirt. Her nervous behavior. There was no way Libby was going to calmly come up with a plan to fix this. A bead of sweat dropped to his desk. Empathy sweat.

At the front of the room, Cindy leaned over and whispered at Libby. "Hey, Lib . . ." She cut her eyes back, making sure Mr. Everett wasn't watching. "How's your campaign planning coming along?"

Libby clenched her fists under her desk. "Fine, you know, perfect. Also, fine." *Wow, I sound like a genius.*

"I hear the two of us are the only ones running." Cindy lifted a brow. "Should make for a good race." She rested her elbow on her desk and sunk her chin into her palm. "And I hear Trevor's your manager. Again?"

Libby accidentally dropped her pencil to the floor. "Yep. Like always."

She leaned down to pick up the dropped pencil, suddenly feeling nervous. It was Cindy's line of questioning. Was she trying to imply that hiring Trevor year after year wasn't such a good idea? Immediately, this all brought back the haunting memory of the Horrifying Incident of the Sixth Grade Student Council Campaign. The one where she lost the election to Cindy—the one where her loss wasn't due to a pattern *at all*.

At that time in sixth grade, Trevor was suffering from a serious dry-erase marker allergy. Or so he assumed. There had been a three-page article in the local newspaper on the dangers of certain smells and how they can cause sinus inflammation, and dry-erase markers had been included on the very, very long list. So he convinced (begged) Libby to make her whole campaign center around the eradication of dry-erase markers in the classroom. Libby tried to explain to him (begged) that he shouldn't ask her to do it because dry-erase markers were simply a part of the everyday learning environment and that she needed to focus on issues like playground equipment and cleaning up school grounds. But Trevor sneezed and complained of headaches until she finally agreed (caved) and supported his Dry-Erase Marker Removal Program.

Rumor has it, she lost because of her slogan.

FROM THE ARCHIVES: PHOTO OF LIBBY, SIXTH GRADE

Some say it was the use of a triple rhyme that cost her the election—certainly *no one* likes a triple rhyme—but Libby knew deep down that the dry-erase marker idea would never win the hearts of a 51 percent majority. But Trevor had asked her to do it for him, so she did, because that's what best friends do.

Cindy had won in a landslide. Her platform that year

was based on antibullying—always a popular issue. In fourth grade, Libby had built her campaign around the benefits of more recess (exercise causing increased attention span); she'd handily won the election.

But Libby had made a misstep last year, and she had to make sure she didn't again.

She placed her pencil back on her desk, hoping this conversation with Cindy was over. But that's when Cindy sighed—it was a fake sigh, the kind where someone breathes in and out dramatically and waits for someone to ask them about it. Cindy had seen it on TV.

"What is it, Cindy?" Libby asked, getting the feeling the answer was probably something she didn't want to hear.

"Oh! Just all this talk of a manager," Cindy gasped. "I don't have one this year, actually."

"You don't?!" Libby couldn't believe it. Cindy wasn't prepared this close to the election?

But Cindy wiggled in her seat and grinned, unable to hold in the news she couldn't wait to unload on Libby. "I don't have a manager . . . I have a team! Team Cindy! And we always use an exclamation point after our name. Cute, right?!"

Libby clutched her stomach. "Wait. So you *do* have a campaign figured out?"

Cindy bounced and wiggled in her seat even more. She glanced at Mr. Everett, making sure he was still busy. "For sure! And Team Cindy! has a synchronized cheer planned for later this week. And we're thinking about starting an interactive Web forum for all my fans to chat! And we have matching pom-poms! So what about you? Do you have lots of plans?"

"Me? Plans?" Libby gripped the sides of her desk to keep from falling out of it. She turned and looked at Trevor. When she'd seen him at the bus stop less than an hour earlier, he had been a picture of cool. But now? Not so much—he was sweating and his book was upside down.

Libby shook her head and turned to face the front. Was it possible for Trevor to help her come up with a cool campaign?

A plan, she thought. A big, crazy plan is what I need if I'm ever going to stand a chance of winning this election.

Then she took a deep breath and let out her best fake sigh, one she'd seen on TV.

"What is it, Lib?" Cindy asked.

"Me? Just all this talk of campaign plans. I have plans all right . . . *lots* of them."

Trevor Jones

Drinking from the
water fountain

8:49 a.m.

I sweated so much in that last class, I think I may have lost some weight. Feeling a little dehydrated right now.

[takes a long sip of water from the fountain, wipes mouth with the back of his hand]

Okay, so anyway. I don't know what those two said to each other, but at the very end I noticed Libby perked up a bit.

Maybe Molly was right? Maybe Libby really did figure out a plan!

Whatever it is, as her manager, I'll do whatever she needs to make it work. But right now I'm still pretty dehydrated. That was a lot of empathy sweat.

[goes back to drinking from the fountain]

Libby Gardner

Outside the door of
Mr. Everett's class

Fidgety

8:50 a.m.

I tried. I did. For those first few minutes of class I pulled out a piece of paper and tried to come up with some awesome ideas for a campaign.

But for some reason, Luke telling me my campaign has to be cool has caused me to come down with Candidate's Block. I can't think of a single catchy, viral, informative platform. Nothing!

So when Cindy told me about her plans for Team Cindy with an exclamation point, and when I saw Trevor sweating like that . . . I realized I had to do something drastic.

I can't compete with Cindy's coordination of T-shirts and pom-poms—not this late in the game. No, if I'm going to defeat Cindy, I'm going to have to go in the opposite direction of her. I need someone who will help me think about things differently.

So I'm going to ask for help from an unlikely source.

[takes a deep breath, clasps hands together]

I'm going to ask Molly Decker to manage my campaign.

CHAPTER FOUR

MOLLY DECKER.

Daughter of the vice principal. Frequent weekend user of Chunky Cobalt #7 hair highlighting kit. Fan of dark colors—*all* of them (except for maroon—a little too peppy).

She had been Trevor's date for the fall dance, but she had turned out to not be the best choice. Trevor discovered that Molly had snuck into the gym and replaced all the healthy snacks with Zingers and orange soda. The chaos had been epic. And whether Libby, as party committee chairperson, was responsible for the mess or not, she had felt bad that the dance had been ruined.

Even though Molly had taken the blame and served her detention and had even made friends with Trevor,

Libby was still a little nervous around her—Molly was a rather prickly person, and that didn't seem to be changing anytime soon.

However, Libby figured asking Molly to be her campaign manager might be the smartest idea she'd had yet.

Molly was intelligent.

Molly got right to the point.

Molly had multiple school district experience.

And Molly could be cruel.

She's perfect for campaign management, Libby thought. Plus, she hates glitter and pep, so she'll come up with a campaign totally different than Cindy's.

After they were dismissed from homeroom, Libby waited patiently by her locker until she saw Molly pass by. There were five minutes in between classes—the perfect amount of time to casually walk up to Molly at her locker, ask her the question, and get to class.

But she noticed that farther down the hall, Trevor was fumbling through his books. Her chest tightened. Trevor wasn't just some kid going through his locker; he was her best friend and her campaign manager—the one she'd had since fourth grade. How could she do this to him?

Except last year's campaign hadn't worked out so well; doing him that favor had caused her to lose the election.

But maybe this time he could come up with some ideas that worked? Shouldn't she at least give him the chance? Before she could continue with these questions in her head, Cindy bounced up to her.

She was happy to see Libby just standing there in the hallway because she was ready to move into phase two of her plan. The part where she got into her opponent's head by making her worried she would never win. And Cindy knew *exactly* what would make Libby worried. "Check it out, Lib. Just like I was telling you. Team Cindy with an exclamation point! We even have our own headquarters!"

Cindy threw her hands in the air to add some dramatic flair. "You won't believe how much work I've put into it. Team Cindy! Headquarters is my biggest project yet. I'm so proud!" She knew overhyping was a smart tactic to use in order to plant a seed of doubt.

Judging from the pale color that had spread across Libby's face, Cindy could tell it was starting to work.

Time to seal the deal. Or pour water on the seed. Or whatever.

Cindy grabbed Libby's arm and pulled her down the hall—it was sort of a friendly pull, but also sort of . . . *not*. Then, as if in a dramatic slow-motion film scene, Libby took in a sight that made her instantly queasy.

Cindy's locker.

Libby couldn't even speak. Cindy's campaign headquarters had a *chandelier*?! All she had were some markers and campaign posters in a trash can, and last-minute plans that required guts she didn't have.

But that chandelier.

Cindy hadn't just gone into serious campaigning mode, this was *Mega Professional* Campaigning Mode. Libby felt the class presidency—her dream—starting to slip away from her. No, no, no . . . she couldn't let this happen.

She pressed her lips together tightly and bolted down the hallway, past Trevor and right up to Molly. Suddenly, from out of nowhere, she had the guts she needed. She was going to ask Molly Decker to be the best campaign manager Westside Middle School had ever seen.

She'd let Trevor be a manager too—he could staple pamphlets and give pep talks. And she'd apologize to him later. After all, this wasn't personal; this was politics. Hopefully he'd understand.

Libby marched up to Molly and blurted out, "Um. You. Could . . . I have a question!" Great, Libby thought. I sound *so* sane.

"Ask it, then." Molly didn't look Libby in the eye; she was too busy fiddling with a safety pin stuck to her jacket. Molly had already made an effort to be friends with Trevor—did she really need to be friends with Libby, too? Having more than one friend sounded exhausting.

Libby motioned for Molly to come across the hall and out of earshot of Trevor; he'd certainly become suspicious if he saw the two of them speaking. Except talking with Molly wasn't such an easy task, due to her spiky-as-a-prickly-pear-cactus personality.

"Can I ask you"—Libby's voice quivered a little—"a question?"

Advanced Calculus = Difficult   Talking to Molly = Just As Difficult

HOLA! Kitty Cat!

"Ask. It," Molly replied, not hiding that she was annoyed with Libby for asking if she could ask a question. GET ON WITH IT, ALREADY was Molly's general life motto.

But Libby noticed that other kids were starting to look at them due to the strangeness of their conversation—or *lack* of conversation—and she also noticed Trevor was now watching them, too. The hall wasn't the place to do this. She turned her body so Trevor couldn't hear, and whispered, "How about we talk at lunch?"

Molly shrugged. "Sounds life-changing."

"Great!" Libby said. Though she hadn't exactly accomplished what she'd set out to—specifically, to ask Molly to be her campaign manager—she'd at least taken a step in the right direction by arranging a lunch meeting. Finally, the heaviness that had been in her chest all morning felt a little bit lighter.

Trevor kept peeking at Libby and Molly, wondering what was going on between them. But then he figured he should focus on the list he'd spent most of homeroom working on. It contained all his plans for fixing Libby's campaign. He couldn't wait to show her.

He figured he'd take it on himself to come up with a cool campaign since he knew a thing or two about being cool and all the effort it took. And so far, even though it was only 8:52 a.m., he was making it through the day with his popularity intact just fine. Which made him the perfect person to run her campaign.

Funny slogans, he thought. That's what will get Libby the votes.

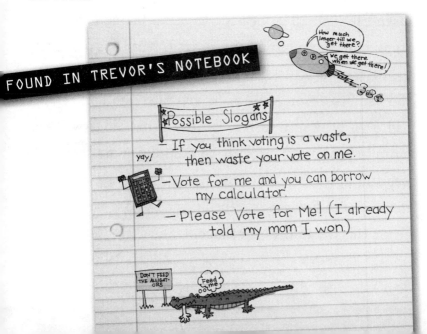

FOUND IN TREVOR'S NOTEBOOK

How much longer till we get there?
We get there when we get there!

Possible Slogans

— If you think voting is a waste, then waste your vote on me.
yay!

—Vote for me and you can borrow my calculator.

— Please Vote for Me! (I already told my mom I won.)

DON'T FEED THE ALLIGATORS
Feed me

"It's gotta be funnier," Marty said, peering over his shoulder.

"I just realized that." Trevor crumpled his paper.

"And if you can't think of something funny, go bizarre."

"Why bizarre?"

"A bizarre slogan forces your voter to think, which makes him feel more intelligent. Always make your voter think he's smart, even if he's not," Marty explained as he snacked on a bag of corn nuts. "And always give away free stuff. Everyone likes stuff. Later, dude."

Trevor watched as Marty sauntered off, and thought maybe Marty would make a good campaign manager. The confidence, the good advice, the casual walking—all the makings of a solid manager.

But then Trevor's eyes fixed on another sight farther down the hall: Libby heading to class, taking long, sleek steps, looking unhurried and relaxed. What was going on?

He was speechless. Because—if he wasn't mistaken—she had just taken Molly aside and talked to her. Perhaps had even been *nice* to her. It wasn't that Libby was ever *mean* to people; it's just that he was fully aware that Libby was still upset that Molly had ruined the dance, and being friendly with her was as difficult as advanced calculus.

So this is weird, Trevor thought. Something is going on.

Cindy Applegate

Buffing out smudges on the chandelier hanging in Team Cindy! Headquarters

8:56 a.m.

Sure, I was trying to get Libby nervous for Thursday's debate. Normally she doesn't get all that worried when I start up with my precampaign intimidation. I mean, I do it to anyone who tries to run against me. But this year, intimidating Libby seems different. It seems to be . . . WORKING. Did you see how she ran away when I showed her my headquarters?

But okay, I'm sort of somewhat completely interested in what these so-called "plans" are that Libby has for her campaign. Because her old-school strategies won't win her this election. She's even using Trevor as her manager again. What is she thinking? It's common knowledge that he convinced her to base her entire sixth grade campaign on dry-erase markers. I mean, dry-erase markers? REALLY? Next thing you know she'll be up there at Thursday's debate talking about how the smell of Magic Markers causes hives. Even though—honestly—I think those blueberry-smelling ones totally do. Congress needs to outlaw those. But JUST blueberry because the root beer ones ROCK. For reals.

Libby Gardner

Sipping water from
the fountain

Looking quite
relaxed

8:57 a.m.

I can't use my old ways of thinking to win this election.

Molly is the wild card. She's mysterious and ripped and torn and, yeah, I'm completely scared of her.

I just have to get the guts to talk to her at lunch and convince her to be my campaign manager. The best campaign manager Westside Middle School has ever seen.

Plus, Trevor will be busy eating with Jake Jacobs and his crew—he'll be distracted and won't even notice me talking with Molly. It's perfect!

Lunchtime . . . me and Molly . . . this will work.

Molly Decker

7th grader
Still in the hall
Totally confused
by the previous
conversation
8:59 a.m.

Um. I have no idea why Libby wants to talk to me at lunch. Maybe she wants to demand some sort of apology from me for the fall dance incident? I don't know why that would matter to her. Everything turned out fine in the end—I mean, I was the one who got the detention. But she still seems all weird around me, so whatever.

I'm not going to apologize to her—what's done is done. Maybe it's best if I just stay away at lunch. Sneak out or something. That's what I'll do.

I prefer to avoid things.

CHAPTER FIVE

LATER THAT MORNING IN HISTORY CLASS, **L**IBBY HAPPILY sat next to Trevor and smiled as if everything was looking up. After all, it really was. She had a plan and the confidence needed to actually go through with it.

But that's when the intercom crackled.

"Students, there is a list of rules to be followed when it comes to running student class elections," Vice Principal Decker announced. "And since I am in charge of all events in which students are involved, Principal Stine has put me in charge of the election committee. Principal Stine is still on his PhD research trip studying the effects of warm weather on student learning, so he won't return from Maui until next month." He cleared his throat. "Anyway. According to rule number seven point two dash three of the student handbook, there must be a minimum of three candidates for each position. But, as of right now, we only have two students running for seventh grade class president: Cindy Applegate and Libby Gardner. Which means if no one else decides to run by the end of today, we will cancel that position, and the eight grade class president will oversee all of student council. Which has never happened in the history of our school. So if you would like to run against Cindy and Libby, please come see me. Thank you and have a great day, Westside!"

Trevor swallowed hard. There was no way he could have a great day. *Cancel* the seventh grade class president election? If there was no election, Libby would be devastated. Plus, he was just about to come up with some seriously funny, cool slogans—he was certain of it. Surely he could find someone to run against them. Except that might prove to be a challenging task.

Since the fourth grade, only Marnie Steiner had ever attempted to go up against Libby and Cindy. And she had dropped out after the second day of campaigning once she realized the two of them took this campaigning stuff perhaps a bit too seriously. Laminated posters, glossy brochures, bumper stickers, yard signs, focus groups, street teams, cold calls, you name it. Not to mention serious passion. Marnie had tried to keep up, but she simply couldn't take the pressure. No one could.

When they were dismissed from class, Trevor watched as Libby raced out ahead of him. This was not a good sign—Vice Principal Decker's announcement had clearly upset her.

He spotted Libby in the hall and rushed over. "Don't pull out the ranch dressing. We can figure this out."

Libby was known to turn to ranch dressing when she was worried or sad or bored. Truth be told, sometimes she even pulled out the ranch dressing if it was a little foggy outside.

"There's no way to fix this," she said. "No one will run against Cindy and me. It's a hopeless case."

"In just thirty seconds, you're giving up?"

Essentially, Trevor was right. She had given up. Libby felt the whole election had suddenly gone from difficult to impossible. She needed to create a whole new "cooler than cool" campaign from scratch, convince Molly Decker to be her manager, and now find SOMEONE—a real live person—to run against her and Cindy by the end of the day?!

Libby opted for giving up.

She crossed her arms and tried to explain the situation in a calm voice. "No one has run against us since Marnie

Steiner, and she only lasted two days. I have no campaign planned. I don't have a slogan. All my posters are in the trash. This day is historically awful. I think giving up is exactly the right choice."

"Let's face one awful thing at a time. I'll find someone to run against you. All we need is a seventh grader with a beating heart. I can find *that*. After all, I'm kind of popular now . . . I'm sure I can convince someone to run."

Libby leaned against her locker, narrowing her eyes at him, unsure if he was up to the task. "But do you think you can find someone who will not only run against us but will also be willing to lose? Though, I'll be honest with you, since I have no idea how to win this election, it's not going to take much to beat me." She waved him off. "No. You don't have to do this. Maybe class president just isn't in my future. Maybe this is a sign or something."

"Have you eaten some bad food? Swallowed some poison?"

"I'm serious. Let's just call it off."

"Did you hit your head in a bizarre fall? Because you are *not* sounding like yourself."

"Forget it, Trevor," she said. "It's not going to work out for me."

He could tell he wasn't getting through to her. So he

quickly eyebrowed her a message—left then right with a twitch at the end: *You can do this.*

Since they'd been friends forever, Libby immediately knew what he meant. But she wasn't sure whether to believe him.

"You can eyebrow messages to me all day, but it doesn't change how I feel."

Trevor threw his hands in the air. "You just need to have confidence."

She started to walk off, but looked back and said in a weak voice, "I wish I did." And then she disappeared around the corner.

Trevor didn't know why Libby was so unconfident, but *he* wasn't going to give up. He'd find someone—with or without her permission—because that's what good campaign managers do.

He hoped.

So he went off in search of a "person" with no "personality" and no "witty slogan," with just a "beating heart," to run for seventh grade president.

In art class, he approached Jamie Jennison—a girl he'd once mistaken for a guy—which, luckily, she didn't bring up. His newfound popularity must have helped her look past all that now.

But convincing her to run for president was a no-go. "Pfft. There's no way I'd win." She laughed him off. "Libby is the best candidate, and she'll have some sort of amazing campaign that *no one* can beat. The girl was born for that job."

Moving on, in math, Trevor reluctantly walked up to Nancy Polanski—a girl who had expressed her crush on him by punching him in the stomach. Nancy thought he was cool even before the Corey Long hair-drenching incident, so this was going to be easy. Though he couldn't help but hope that she'd developed a crush on someone else and wouldn't punch him when he tried to start up a friendly conversation about whether she'd run for student class president.

"Nope," Nancy said. "Even if I wanted to be president—which I don't—Cindy is sure to win. Her dad will probably help her put out yard signs again this year. And my guess is her campaign will have something to do with gum chewing, which helps me concentrate when I'm exercising. So she has my vote." And then before walking off, she proved yet again that she did, in fact, still have a crush on him.

Trevor wished she would find a new way of expressing herself. One that didn't involve physical pain.

Later on in health class, and still in quite a bit of pain

Her form continues to improve.

Maybe this is why they call it a "CRUSH"?

from Nancy's love slug, Trevor asked the Baker twins if one of them would run for president. The Baker twins, Brian and Brad, were known for relentless bickering over which one had "more" of something.

"Dude, you have more pencils. Give me one," Brian said to Brad.

"No, Mom gave us the same number. You must have lost one."

Trevor cleared his throat. "So. The seventh grade class president? Would one of you want to run?"

"But your green pencil is better. Give me that one," Brian said.

"Guys? Remember me? The one who drenched Corey Long with orange soda? You know . . . Trevor?" He waved a hand in front of their faces, wondering if he was invisible.

"Give me back my blue one," Brad said.

Trevor leaned in. "Seriously, one of you should run. Clearly you're both opinionated. And focused."

"Give me my pencil."

"Give me *my* pencil."

Trevor was actually relieved when health class finally ended so he could escape their arguing. There had to be a better choice.

As he headed to his locker, he heard a familiar voice.

"Watch that posture."

It was Wilson, the janitor who shall not be called the janitor. He patted Trevor on the back. "Slumping like that tells me you're either having a rough day or you need more orange juice."

"Rough day, Wilson. Can you help me out? If I can't find someone to run against Libby and Cindy for class president, an eighth grader has to take over. But I can't find anyone to run against them."

"How many people have you asked?"

"Three. Well, four since they're twins."

"Then you haven't tried everyone. And stand up straight. You need more orange juice," Wilson said as he walked on.

Trevor looked up and down the hall, studying the students. He noticed one lone girl standing near the water fountain. She was dressed in red jeans and a sweater vest, and she wore chunky black glasses and an extremely clean pair of Keds tennis shoes.

Marnie Steiner.

Since she'd run against them once before, Trevor figured he might be able to convince her to do it again. "Marnie!" he yelled out as he raced toward her.

But she whirled around and sprinted away from him full-force down the hall.

Marnie Steiner

7th grader
Hiding out in the
library, completely
out of breath

12:02 p.m.

No. Flipping. Way. Absolutely not. Don't even get me started about it.

Okay, fine. Here's what happened. Last year, I entered the race, but Cindy started hounding me relentlessly with questions about my campaign. What was my slogan? My color theme? My texture theme? Did I have backup singers? Celebrity endorsements?

The intimidation . . . it wouldn't STOP.

I had nightmares about running for office—which turned into night sweats, which turned into sleepwalking, which turned into sleep eating—and I had to pull out of the race after only TWO days. I had completely wiped out our snack pantry at midnight one night without realizing it. My mom was really ticked when all her chocolate Twizzlers went missing.

So there's no way Trevor can convince me to go through that nightmare again. I don't think he'll find ANYONE who will.

I'm going to tell Libby she should just forget about it and give up.

Libby Gardner

Getting her lunch
from her locker

12:03 p.m.

Give up? No way. Not now! Did you hear what Trevor
did today? He went behind my back, that sneak!

[big grin]

Such a friend. He's been trying to find someone
to run against me and Cindy, and I heard he even
tried to chase down Marnie Steiner. So sweet!

I bet if he keeps at it, he'll find SOMEONE by
the end of the day who's willing to run against
us.

There may just be a little glimmer of hope
forming, which means I need to put my plan back
into action. Molly Decker is going to become my
manager, and this presidency will be mine.

Oh, right. I also need to come up with a slogan.
And a platform. And make new posters.

[clenches stomach]

CHAPTEЯ SIX

IT WAS A FEW MINUTES BEFORE LUNCH, AND **T**REVOR realized he'd just spent half a day trying to find someone to run against Cindy and Libby and hadn't experienced a smidge of luck. His popularity didn't seem to be helping like he thought it would. He didn't know where to turn.

But then he remembered something in his backpack. His Mystical 7 Ball. Trevor's Magic 8 Ball had been lost in an unfortunate driveway accident. "Sorry, I didn't see it when I was backing up," his mother had explained, and then quickly replaced it for him. Except Ms. Jones was quite a thrifty shopper and purchased a generic knockoff brand.

Standing in the hall, looking left and right to make sure no one was watching, Trevor slyly pulled out his

Mystical 7 Ball. Cautiously, he shook it while asking a question. "Will someone run against Libby and Cindy for student class president?"

Before he could read the answer, Molly walked up behind him and tugged on his shirt. "Why are you asking a ball questions?"

He twirled around. "Me? No. I'm not—"

"Look, I've seen this before—I've been to *lots* of schools. When a guy is whispering questions at a ball, it means he's worried about something. I knew this one kid from Lincoln who based all his decisions on a mood ring."

"And what happened to him?" Trevor winced.

"Let's not go there." She folded her arms and raised a brow. "So? What's with the ball?"

He lowered his head. "It's a Mystical Seven Ball. It gives you answers."

She nodded like she understood. "Hank Hoffman from Jefferson Elementary, he did the same thing, too. Never knew why, though. . . ." She strummed her fingers on her arm and waited for Trevor to give an explanation. Not that she felt he *owed* her an explanation, but it was just that the day had been pretty boring so far and this was the most interesting part yet.

Trevor sighed. He *had* to tell Molly exactly what was

going on—first because she looked bored and everyone knew Molly got up to no good when things weren't interesting. And second, she'd actually been attempting to become friends with him—something he knew didn't come easy to her. So he appreciated the effort she was making.

"Here's the truth," he said. "I only break it out in emergencies. I wasn't planning on actually using it—that was the old me. Now that I've gotten popular since the Corey Long incident, I found out I have to do whatever it takes to *stay* popular. Apparently I can't make one mistake or it could all go away."

Molly shuddered like he was telling a ghost story. "You really believe all that?"

"Libby's cousin says it's true. And now I can't even convince anyone to run in the election, so maybe I was wrong—I'm not as cool as I thought I was."

She shook her head and said softly, "I doubt that you're not cool anymore, Trevor."

The bell rang for the start of lunch.

Trevor reached into his locker to grab his paper lunch bag, then hesitated. He'd been eating his lunch from home all week without putting any thought into it. But today was different. Today he would be eating at Jake Jacobs's table. What if they ate only school lunches? Would they mock his brown-bag lunch? What if this ended up being the "one big mistake" and he became a laughingstock?

"I'm going to ask the ball if I should eat this sandwich," he said. "I'm not sure if it's cool to eat lunch from home or from the cafeteria. What do the popular kids do?" Trevor stopped, realizing how this all sounded. He shook his head. "This is ridiculous, right? I'm worrying about ridiculous things. And I'm going to ruin my reputation with this ridiculous mystical ball. You think I'm ridiculous?"

"Use the ball, Trevor."

"But everyone will—"

Molly held up her hand, stopping him. "Go ahead and use it for as many decisions as you want. Do it because you know it's *not* cool, and you don't care. Because, guess what? That's the *definition* of cool."

Wow, Trevor thought. He'd never heard Molly use so many words together in the form of sentences that then formed a paragraph—a *nice* paragraph. He suddenly felt a little comfortable with this idea of using the magic ball. Like he'd do whatever she said. It was those eyes, he figured.

"You mean just ask the ball a question . . . right here . . . in this busy hallway . . . so everyone can see that this is how I make my decisions?"

Molly grabbed the ball from him and held it out in the palm of her hand. "Just ask."

Trevor shook the ball. "Should I eat this tuna sandwich?"

Molly took the ball back, turned it toward her, and read the answer out loud. "Nope." She looked up at him, a little surprised the ball had taken such a sassy tone.

"The Mystical Seven Ball is a bit . . . casual," he explained.

"Well, then it sounds like it's chicken nuggets for you, Trevor Jones."

He blushed, glancing around to see who was laughing at him. But, strangely enough, kids were just going about their business. A few of them even gave him a smile.

Maybe Molly was right, he thought. No one thought it was weird. Using the ball because it wasn't cool actually *was* cool.

Molly leaned in. "But snag the soda from your lunch. All the cool kids eat the school's lunch and bring their drinks from home—the school only sells milk, *warm* milk."

He smirked at her. "So the next time I need advice, can I just ask you? Instead of an inanimate object?"

She looked away. "Nah. Stick with that sassy ball."

Satisfied that cafeteria chicken nuggets were the perfect choice for him, Trevor grabbed his soda, threw his sack lunch to the back of his locker, and slammed the door. "Let's go eat."

"Sure," Molly said. "But I'm supposed to meet Libby for lunch. She wants to ask me a question. Which is weird."

Trevor wondered what this was all about. "You're right. It's very weird."

Molly Decker

Outside the
cafeteria, smiling
(slightly)

12:05 p.m.

So I convinced Trevor to use that Mystical Seven
Ball to make his decisions. For a minute there, he
thought he should ask ME for advice, but really
. . . it's more fun if he relies on that ball.
Because, get this . . . that kid Hank Hoffman? The
one from Jefferson Elementary School who based
all his decisions on a magic ball? The COOLEST
things started happening in that school. The fire
department showed up, a cow got loose, they had to
repaint the outside of the building—I have no idea
why. But it. Was. Awesome.

And here I thought this was going to be a REGULAR
NUMBINGLY BORING Monday at Westside.

Finally things are getting interesting.

[nods approvingly]

Finally.

CHAPTER SEVEN

LUNCH. **T**REVOR WAS DREADING IT, AND YET *NOT* dreading it. This was because he was being pulled by two conflicting feelings. On the one side, there was the strangeness of Libby suddenly wanting to talk with Molly. The two of them weren't friends, so he wondered what she was up to. It wasn't like Libby to keep secrets from him—she was as straightforward as a two-by-four plank.

But on the other side, there was awesomeness. Today was the day he was going to sit with Jake Jacobs and his crew. A feat he never thought possible through his own actions. But, no. He was going to sit with the most popular kids in seventh grade, and all on his own doing. Now all he had to do was get through lunch without making any mistakes and messing up his reputation.

So lunch was going to be a mix of strange and awesome, and he wasn't sure which one was going to win out.

Trevor and Molly went through the line and grabbed their food. Trevor was not aware that Molly's plan was to grab her lunch and bolt, and so he was confused when Molly started moving toward the cafeteria exit. Still, despite the sound of hundreds of kids laughing and screaming, Trevor was able to hear Libby's voice when she called out for Molly.

"Over there. Libby's waving at you," Trevor said. Except instead of walking over to Libby's table, Molly quickened her pace and was beelining out the back door in the wrong direction. "Molly!" Trevor called out as he ran up behind her. "You're going the wrong way." He grabbed her by the shoulders and turned her back into the direction of the chaotic cafeteria, directing her toward Libby. "She's sitting right over there. She probably just wants to talk about what happened at the dance. But who knows?" Truth was, *he* really wanted to know.

Molly thought for sure her plan to avoid the situation by sneaking out and hiding in the bathroom would work, but apparently Trevor was not reading her body language—that "rushing off to an alternative location" would have made her much happier at that moment. But it was too late. Libby had cleared a spot and was pulling out a seat, waiting for Molly to join her.

Trevor figured he would give them "space" to "talk." Which made him "nervous." "Very." For some reason, he felt maybe they were going to talk about him. Or what had happened at the dance. Or both. Surely they weren't talking about fashion; Libby preferred her clothes sewn, while Molly thought the more torn the better.

But then his curiosity got to him—he had to know. He pulled Molly by the elbow straight up to Libby's table.

"Hi, Trevor." Libby tilted her head, looking confused. "Aren't you supposed to be at Jake's table?"

"Yeah, I'm on my way." He narrowed his eyes. "Sooo . . . you two are eating together?"

Libby pressed her lips together and her eyes grew big, looking like she'd just swallowed something extra large. "Yep," she finally said.

Trevor crossed his arms. "What are you going to talk about?"

Libby couldn't believe he was being this nosy. "Just stuff. We're talking about . . . girl stuff." She knew saying "girl stuff" would get him to leave them alone.

Trevor blushed and turned around. "Have fun," he said, as he quickly walked away. He wasn't quite sure what they were going to talk about, but he *did* know that "girl stuff" was a phrase he didn't want to be anywhere near.

Molly flopped into the chair and rested her chin in her hand, looking bored. "You wanted to talk to me? And please tell me we're not actually going to talk about girl stuff."

Libby smiled and laced her fingers together. Her project-ready stance. Also her nervous-about-asking-Molly-this-question stance. It was a stance that worked in many situations.

She took a deep breath and glanced up, but that's when she saw Trevor wandering over to the other side of the room. And suddenly her stomach sank. He'd been trying so hard to be a good campaign manager—he'd stapled pamphlets, attempted pep talks, and spent half the day trying to find another candidate. How could she ask Molly to be her manager too and crush his feelings like that?

But wait. Libby realized there might be a way around this moral problem.

"Molly, I want to win seventh grade class president," she declared.

"Fascinating."

"But we still need one more person to run against me and Cindy."

Molly looked confused. "Wait . . . are you asking *me* to run?"

Libby hadn't considered that option. She quickly played out a number of scenarios in her mind and concluded that wasn't a good idea. Molly's straight-to-the-point demeanor and slightly negative attitude was much better suited for management. "No, no. I was thinking maybe instead of Trevor running my campaign, you might . . ."

"You want me to be your campaign manager."

Score! Libby wasn't even going to have to ask the question—Molly was practically offering to be her manager! She'd explain to Trevor that she'd had to hire Molly to be her campaign *co*-manager since she couldn't possibly say no to Molly's offer, as she was being "friendly," which was in her "nature," and turning down her offer would have been "rude." A win-win, no hurt feelings.

"So you're going to be my campaign manager!"

"I wasn't offering, I was *clarifying*."

"Oh." Libby dropped her shoulders, realizing that escaping this moral problem wasn't going to happen so easily. "Look, I'd like you to be my manager. What do you say? And if you don't mind, could you maybe not tell Trevor about any of this?" If Molly agreed to be her manager, Libby knew she'd have to break the news to him at the right time. She just wasn't sure when that right time was.

Molly had no idea why Libby wanted to keep all this from Trevor. But clearly it was important to her that she have Molly—out of everyone—as her campaign manager. Which she thought was pretty nice, actually. And since Molly had made a pact with her father to try to become "somewhat friendlier," she figured why not? She pushed out her hand and said, "You have yourself a deal."

After grabbing a tray of chicken nuggets, Trevor spotted Jake and his crew sitting on the far side of the room in their

FOUND SCRIBBLED ON THE BACK
OF MOLLY'S LUNCH NAPKIN

This day

Half full
(of black tar)
but still...
half full.
Things looking up.

usual spot with one seat still available at their table. That would normally be a positive thing—a spot left for him! But there was only one problem: their table was directly across from the eighth grade section. And, yep, that meant *right next* to Corey Long's table.

When am I ever going to catch a break? Trevor wondered.

The horror of Libby's chat with her cousin Luke suddenly filled every blood vessel in his body as he clutched his chest. Sure, he had appropriate lunch items . . . a soda from home and a school-bought lunch—but what if it wasn't enough? What if they expected more? Would it be possible for him to maintain his cool, not say anything wrong, nod, smile, fist-bump, and not make a single mistake for the *entire* lunch period?

Keep things simple: just nod, eat quietly, and don't cause a disaster, he coached himself. People do that ALL the time.

Jake Jacobs gave Trevor a slight wave, indicating that he should come sit with him. It was one of those cool kind of hand waves where the movement is fluid—intentional, yet natural—and transitions perfectly into the dunking of a chicken nugget in barbecue sauce. Trevor couldn't believe how cool it was. Did Jake *practice* that? Unbelievable.

Trevor was still in disbelief that he was being invited to sit with these guys. So no matter how close they were to Corey Long, he simply had to take this opportunity.

Slipping into the last empty seat, Trevor nodded, waved, then clamped his hands down on his knees to hide the fact that they were bouncing from nervousness. Eventually his knees slowed down a bit, and he got up enough nerve to use one free hand to take a bite of chicken nugget.

Fortunately for Trevor, the kids at the table were already in the middle of a conversation about skateboard parks, and all he had to do was sit and listen as he ate his food. It was going remarkably well.

But then out of his peripheral vision, he noticed something. Movement. Someone at the next table had gotten up and was walking toward them.

Corey Long.

Oh, no. Not now. Not here.

Trevor choked a little on a piece of chicken nugget and started to cough.

"You okay, bro?" Jake asked.

Trevor's eyes filled with tears from the coughing. "Yep," he finally wheezed.

Trevor decided to look away and stare at the exit sign

hanging over the door. He figured extreme lack of eye contact was the best alternative at this point. He didn't want Corey to see that he was crying—Corey would never believe it was from chicken-nugget choking. Plus, what evil thing could Corey possibly do to an innocent kid staring at an exit sign?

Corey made his way around the table, and noticed that Trevor was sitting at Jake Jacobs's table for the first time. Since this was probably a pretty big moment for Trevor, considering how popular Jake was—at least for a seventh grader—Corey figured this would be a *very* good time to get back at him for the orange soda incident.

He considered pouring a soda on Trevor's head, but decided that was too obvious, not creative enough. Just repeating what someone did to you was pretty lame. So Corey opted for a trick his older brother had pulled on him one time . . . the shaken soda maneuver.

As he approached Trevor, he realized just how easy this was going to be. For some reason, Trevor was staring off in the opposite direction. He quietly snuck up behind him, pretended to drop something, and then reached into Trevor's backpack and shook up his soda with all his might. This was going to be one massive explosion. Corey then casually walked on and stood over on the far side of the room to get the best view of the soda fireworks that were about to happen.

"So the Westside skate park"—Jake tapped on the table to get Trevor's attention—"it's the best, bro."

Trevor turned back toward Jake, then realized he didn't see Corey out of his peripheral vision anymore. He looked left, then right, even behind his seat, but no Corey—he was gone. *Whew. Staring at the exit sign worked!*

Trevor was relieved that he was now going to be able to sit and eat lunch in peace. He sat forward and nodded at Jake as if he knew all about skate parks, then calmly pulled the soda out of his backpack, and opened it.

Now, normally this would be an uneventful moment since it's a procedure that he and many people around the world perform on a daily basis. But unfortunately for Trevor, opening his soda turned into an episode on the Science Channel.

The soda spewed out of the bottle—and not just like a volcano, but a volcano filled with Mentos. And hydrogen peroxide. And bubble bath. And dynamite.

The soda shot up and arched beautifully—like a Hawaiian soda rainbow—and splattered all over the floor.

At that moment, Cindy Applegate and her campaign team walked by, all wearing the same T-shirt, which read

ONLY FOUR MORE DAYS UNTIL THE DEBATE, Y'ALL! VOTE FOR CINDY! They were discussing Cindy's election strategy and not paying attention to what had just exploded on the floor.

Cindy stepped into the puddle first. As her right foot slid forward, she instinctively reached out for the nearest Team Cindy! member.

"Help!" Cindy screeched as her feet started to come out from under her.

"Let go of my hair first!"

"Ack!"

"Eeek!"

One Team Cindy! member grabbed on to the other member and then another, creating a human chain to try to help their candidate get steady on her feet. Except that's when they slipped and fell. All of them, like a herd of deer on an ice rink. Arms flailed. Hair flew. Voices shrieked.

The girls were scattered on the floor in a heap of tangled limbs and pink ponytail ribbons. The massive amounts of squeals that ensued caught Vice Principal Decker's attention. He knew that chaos *this* bad could only mean one thing: someone's hair was on fire.

Vice Principal Decker marched over to the red box marked EMERGENCY located high on the wall, and without hesitation, he pulled the lever. The sprinkler system deployed and it doused the whole room for an entire minute—creating a chaotic scene while he announced loudly that everyone should remain very calm.

No one remained very calm. (Except Molly.)

Wilson, the janitor who will not be called a janitor, finally made his way from across the room and shut it off.

But it had drenched the cafeteria workers, Vice Principal Decker, the students, the food, everything. Most of the kids found this hugely entertaining and danced around, enjoying their wet lunchroom. The rest were extremely annoyed. And one was not all that impressed—in fact, was still rather bored.

Cindy pulled herself up off the floor—her naturally curly hair now drippy and long like overcooked spaghetti—and she locked eyes with Trevor. He was still holding the bottle of soda, which was empty but still fizzing, and it became clear to Cindy that this was all his fault.

More than being embarrassed about falling, Cindy was furious. Her campaign T-shirts were beyond ruined. Cindy had ordered the shirts from an overnight printing service she'd found on an Internet site called OvernighT-shirts!com. (Cindy was drawn to any Web site that had an exclamation point in its title.) But OvernighT-shirts!com had seemingly used cheap ink, as the lettering on the girls' T-shirts had

instantly run when the sprinklers doused them.

"NO. WAY. Vice Principal Decker!" Cindy squawked as she raced over to him. "We are NOT walking around the rest of the day with our shirts looking like this! Trevor spilled his soda on *purpose*. That's how I fell, that's why I screamed, that's why the sprinklers went off, and now it's clear he's trying to sabotage my campaign so Libby will win."

"What?! That's not—" Trevor tried to protest.

"I'm lodging a formal complaint, Mr. Decker," Cindy interrupted loudly. "It's not written on paper or anything, but I am formally *complaining*!"

Vice Principal Decker took one look at Cindy's smudged T-shirt and serious scowl and realized that he'd better handle the situation before Cindy *did* find a piece of paper for her complaint. "No need to lodge anything, Cindy. This situation will be handled. There will be a punishment." Vice Principal Decker looked up at Trevor. "Mr. Jones, meet me in my office. Now!"

Wilson

Drying off his tools
with a towel

12:45 p.m.

No sirree, those kids did not need to be doused
with the sprinklers, even though all that shriek-
ing was quite alarming.

I'll tell you what the problem was . . . it
was that soda bottle. In all my many years of
custodial arts, I've NEVER seen such an amazing
spillage of liquid. But that was not your average
spill—it was intentional . . . VERY intentional.
I KNOW soda carbonation, and there was much more
going on there than just Trevor opening a regular
bottle of soda from home.

[lifts a brow]

Like I said . . . I've worked here for many
years—I've seen it all.

Corey Long

8th grader

Outside the cafeteria

Confidently leaning on a wall

12:47 p.m.

What? Did he think I wasn't going to get back at him for dumping orange soda all over me at the dance? My hair still won't do what it's supposed to.

[filmmaker's note: his hair looks fine.]

Honestly, I didn't think I'd get away with it, because usually the person is LOOKING. But Trevor was staring off into space for some reason, and *bam!*, I was able to reach into his backpack and shake the soda, no problem.

It was hilarious! Did you see the way his soda sprayed across the room? And then that sixty-girl pileup on the floor?

[laughs hard while clutching stomach]

And Decker . . . the fire alarm . . . sprinklers . . . Oh, man . . . it HURTS.

[laughs so hard he falls to the floor]

CHAPTER EIGHT

ONE MOMENT **TREVOR JONES WAS SITTING AT THE MOST** popular seventh grade lunch table, and the next he was drenched and sitting in the office face-to-face with the vice principal, who wanted an explanation.

Except he didn't have one.

Trevor couldn't explain what had happened with the soda because he didn't *know* what had happened with the soda. Had he accidentally dropped it just before he opened it and not remembered? Why did it spray like that?

He had no idea, but he figured he should attempt an explanation anyway, because that's what you did when you were face-to-face with the vice principal and he was in that "waiting for an answer" stance.

"See, I've sort of gotten popular since that incident

with Corey Long at the dance," Trevor began. "But I've been having a hard time figuring out this popularity thing, and my palms get all sweaty and clammy. So maybe that's what happened with that soda. Maybe I dropped it sometime and don't remember—which is sorta strange, but I guess it's possible and it's the only explanation I have. I didn't drop it on purpose, sir. I'll try to be more careful next time. And I'll also try to improve my memory."

Vice Principal Decker crossed his arms as he sat behind his desk, thinking this over. "Okay, Trevor. I realize you're under a lot of pressure. But you can't create any more chaos in this school."

Trevor nodded. "No more chaos. Got it."

"But you'll have a punishment. It's a two-pronged punishment."

Anything with the word *punishment* sounded painful to Trevor. Also: *prong*. He flinched.

"First, you're going to spend an hour after school today with the lunch lady."

Ouch. The only redeeming factor of prong one of his punishment was that at least it wasn't an after-school detention, where he'd have to sit with a bunch of other kids in some humiliating fashion. A small victory.

"And the second prong of your punishment . . ."

Trevor scooted to the edge of his chair and hoped for something painless. But he didn't hope hard enough, apparently.

"There's going to be a new rule at Westside: no more sodas."

Well, awesome. Trevor figured the banning of sodas would not only cause his popularity to be obliterated, but he might just become the most hated kid in the history of Westside Middle School.

Vice Principal Decker wished him luck, then handed Trevor a hall pass and sent him on his way to his next class, P.E.

He made his way through the busy hall, and it didn't

take long before he realized that his previously stellar reputation was now at serious risk. Kids were glaring at him—their hair and clothes sopping wet, makeup ruined, shoes squishy. He figured Cindy must have made it clear to everyone that he was to blame for the sprinkler shower, because these looks were so sharp they hurt.

And on top of that, word of the soda ban must have seeped through the office walls, because as he walked toward the P.E. locker room, things were suddenly much different for him. No head nods or smiles or high fives. Mostly all he saw were sneers and all he heard were hushed whispers about no sodas allowed. Trevor dropped his head and kept walking, trying to ignore what was happening.

My ONE mistake was simply opening a bottle of soda? I had no idea it was going to be this easy to wreck my own popularity.

Entering the boys' locker room, Trevor reminded himself to do whatever it took to not make matters any worse. Except the eighth graders were also in the locker room, hurrying to change into their gym clothes, which meant Trevor was about to be face-to-face with Corey Long. Moving more cautiously, Trevor saw Corey, a scowl on his mug, sitting on a bench drying his hair, which had been drenched by the cafeteria sprinklers.

Trevor's heart sped up. The expression on Corey's face was all the evidence he needed to convince him that he had to hide. Turning sideways, Trevor squeezed in between some large eighth graders to get to an open locker. He tossed in his gym uniform and deodorant and decided to wait in a bathroom stall until Corey and all the eighth graders had cleared out before he started dressing. That way, he'd be safe from torment. And also, since the locker room was full of wet seventh and eighth grade guys, the odors were a little too much for his olfactory sense. Meaning: it stunk in there.

The students at Westside were required to bring not only a pair of gold shorts and a royal-blue shirt with the Westside decal, but also a can of deodorant.

In elementary school, deodorant was more of a "personal thing" and not spoken of much. But in middle school, deodorant was spoken about freely and frequently. Because at Westside, no one should feel uncomfortable talking about body odor. At least, that was Counselor Plimp's motto.

As counselor, she was in charge of sending home notices of a sensitive nature. So she was the one who had sent home the reminder notice over the summer about Westside's deodorant policy. Writing sensitive reminder notices was one of her favorite parts of the job.

Dear Parents,

I wanted to bring to your attention that your growing son and/or daughter (but more than likely son) may be experiencing an increase in body odor.

According to "Your Child's Body Is Growing and You Can Accept It!", an increase in body odor is normal and natural and nothing to be ashamed of! In fact, it's something you and your child can someday learn to accept!

However, it is our long-standing policy at Westside to cover up this smell as best as possible so that it does not interfere with our positive learning environment. Or make any of the students nauseous.

Please send your son and/or daughter (but more than likely son) to school with deodorant to be stored in his P.E. locker.

But please, none with a musky fragrance, as Mr. Everett is sensitive to the smell; it gives him a migraine.

Thanks for keeping Westside smelling great!

Miss Plimp

Now, Trevor's mother, being a thrifty shopper, had purchased a jumbo-sized can of Scenty Spice!, a spray deodorant that was a generic off-brand label because (as Ms. Jones would say) smelling good does *not* need to break the bank. She'd even called Miss Plimp to verify the dimensions of the P.E. locker to make sure Trevor's jumbo can of deodorant would fit.

Peeking out from under his stall, Trevor watched as more and more feet exited the locker room. The remaining feet were smaller, more in line with a reasonable seventh grade size. Once he was sure most of the eighth graders had headed out to the gym, he approached his locker—but standing next to it was Jake Jacobs. According to the look on his face, he didn't want to have a cheerful discussion about skate parks.

"Now we can't have sodas because of you?!"

"I didn't mean to—"

"Not cool!"

Jake whirled around as if doing a skate trick and headed over to the far side of the locker room without another word. But it was as if his final words—*not cool*—were hanging over Trevor's head in a cloud puff of shame for everyone to see.

Trevor avoided eye contact with everyone as he removed his uniform and can of discount deodorant from his locker. After getting partially dressed, he reached out to put the deodorant on. Coach Fleming, the seventh grade P.E. teacher, a stocky man with a big smile, happened to be walking by at the time.

In that moment, Trevor learned two glorious lessons. Lesson 1: Generic cans of spray deodorant also have generic spray mechanisms, and Lesson 2: Sometimes generic spray mechanisms don't work right.

Coach Fleming howled in pain.

"Coach! I'm so sorry!" Trevor yelped.

Trevor didn't understand what had gone wrong. His spray deodorant, despite being a discount brand, had always sprayed in the right direction before. But for some reason, on the *one day* he was trying to keep his reputation intact, it suddenly malfunctioned.

It is true, Trevor thought. I will never catch a break.

Coach Fleming had to be rushed to the nurse's office to flush his eyes and mouth out with cold water. Apparently, the coach was highly allergic to something in Trevor's deodorant, which caused a bad case of hives. (And a few bad words, too.)

The eighth graders headed out to the soccer field with Coach Harris, but without Coach Fleming, a substitute teacher was needed. Except there was no substitute teacher available on such short notice for the seventh graders. So the substitute for a substitute was Wilson, the janitor who will not be called a janitor.

"Boys, grab a seat in the gym," he yelled through the door of the P.E. locker room. "We have an announcement."

Grumbling as they finished putting on their uniforms, the seventh grade boys headed out the door.

"This is probably an announcement about you," Jake Jacobs said under his breath to Trevor.

"Me? But it was an accident. Was it really that big of a deal?"

Jake strutted off and didn't answer him. But once they were all seated on the cold floor of the gym, and Trevor got a look at Wilson's face, it was obvious—indeed, it *was* a big deal.

Standing next to Wilson was Vice Principal Decker. "Boys, due to the unfortunate incident that just occurred with Coach Fleming, we are going to have to make a new rule at Westside." Vice Principal Decker cleared his throat and announced loudly to all the boys in Trevor's class, "No more deodorant allowed."

"What?!" everyone gasped.

"No more deodorant? But what about the stick kind? That couldn't hurt anyone," Jake argued.

Vice Principal Decker continued. "We believe Coach Fleming had a reaction to an ingredient in the deodorant. It appears he is severely allergic. Like a peanut allergy, but not—because no one typically *eats* deodorant. But today, unfortunately . . . Coach Fleming did. Sorry, gentlemen, but we can't take any chances. You'll just have to get through your days smelling very much like ripe seventh graders."

The glares and scowls Trevor received from his fellow classmates made him want to disappear. And just before class ended, Jake sauntered up to him, arms folded—no high five in sight. "Don't sit with us at lunch anymore," he said in a low voice, not even bothering to tack the word *bro* to the end of his sentence. Then he walked off, leaving Trevor all alone.

It hit Trevor that in only half a day, his popularity hadn't just been lost . . . it had completely gone down the locker room shower drain.

Trevor Jones

Scuffing his shoes
outside the boys'
locker room
Pretty mad

1:40 p.m.

Aaand that's the end of my newfound popularity.
I'll never doubt Libby's cousin Luke again—looks
like that guy was right about everything.

And who knew Coach Fleming was allergic to alu-
minum chlorohydrate? Not ME, that's for sure. So
is it really MY fault? Surely that one particular
ingredient landing in the man's eyes and mouth was
EVENTUALLY going to happen.

But for some reason, my deodorant nozzle went
haywire and now my popularity has gone out the
door. And I still can't find anyone to run against
Libby and Cindy for student class president. Which
means Libby will be miserable, and therefore I
will be miserable because that's how it works with
best friends.

SURELY it's not possible for this day to get
any worse.

Corey Long

Standing outside
the gym
Unusually excited

1:41 p.m.

Did you hear? The seventh graders can't use deodorant anymore! I mean, is it possible for this day to get any better?!

[laughing, bends over at the waist for a moment]

Gimme a sec . . . I'm okay . . . I'm okay . . .

[finally gains composure]

See, when we were getting ready for gym, Trevor went and HID in the bathroom for some reason. What was he thinking, leaving his locker alone like that??

I couldn't help myself. I pulled the oldest trick in the book. I don't know if it's ACTUALLY the oldest trick in the book; it's just another trick my older brother did to me once. My older brother's kind of a pain. Anyway, I rotated the nozzle on Trevor's deodorant ninety degrees. Yep, the ol' nozzle-turn trick.

Worked perfectly.

Do I feel bad about it? Naw. The dude's gotta stop making it so easy for me.

I'm like the Joker in that movie *The Joker*. No wait . . . he's in *Batman*. The old one with Beetlejuice, not the new one. Except he dies in the last part. So I'm the Joker in the first half of the movie. Yeah . . . I'm First-Half Joker.

Cindy Applegate

Near the boys'
P.E. locker
room, holding
her nose

1:42 p.m.

Do you smell that? Seriously, what IS that smell?

It's like a mixture of boy and bacon and sweat and a video game controller. Or maybe it's more like corn dogs and leather seats and lizards. Whatever it is . . . so gross!

I'm worried a smell like that might make my hair go flat. It's seriously dangerous.

So anyway, about the student class election? I am just going to continue to campaign in the hopes that SOMEONE will join the race and we can get on with this. I'm super positive like that. And meanwhile, I'm happy to report that all the supplies have arrived to start making decorative campaign buttons.

That's right . . . buttons! As far as I know, there is no rule in the handbook about posters and pamphlets being the ONLY thing you can use to get the word out. Not that I've read it.

So, okay. I found these buttons on this Web site called CutestButtonsontheBlock.com, and let me tell you . . . this block has never seen a button like it's about to see.

Everyone's button minds are about to be blown!

[folds arms and wrinkles brows]

I'm not sure if I made any sense there, so you may want to edit that part cuter or something. You can do that, right?

CHAPTER NINE

AFTER **P.E.,** **T**REVOR STOPPED OFF AT HIS LOCKER TO pick up his books and take a moment to lean his forehead against the door in defeat.

This day had won.

He had lost his popularity, and he hadn't found anyone to run for seventh grade class president. Which meant he would become terminally unhappy at the exact same moment that Libby became terminally unhappy. It was like an impending unhappiness tsunami, and he had no idea how to stop it.

But that's when Wilson came down the hall and noticed him resting his forehead against his locker door. "What's wrong, son?"

"Awful day, Wilson. I'm pretty sure I'm doing a terrible

job as Libby's campaign manager. Which won't matter in a couple of hours, considering the race is going to be canceled. Plus, I went from having no reputation to being pretty dang popular to having my popularity suddenly obliterated."

Wilson folded his arms and squinted at him. "How long were you popular?"

"Six point seven days."

"Almost a whole week? That's actually quite good by middle school standards. Believe me, I know these things— I've worked here for many years."

Wilson had a point. Maybe Trevor should be glad for the few days of popularity he *had* had.

Trevor peeled his face off his locker door, wondering if Wilson could help him with the election. "Wilson, you're smart about these things. I need to find someone to run against Cindy and Libby. Marnie Steiner ran away from me. Sprinted, actually. And everyone else I asked refused to do it. I have to get someone to volunteer so we can have the election so that Libby can win. Otherwise, it's going to be a year of misery for her, which means a year of misery for me. Best friends always soak up the misery—it's our duty."

Wilson raised a brow. "So you need someone to run who will not beat Libby?"

"Right. Someone who's a shoo-in to lose. Not very popular, maybe has a past record of doing ridiculous things, and they must be a horrible campaign slogan writer. Someone who says stuff like, 'Vote for me. I know how to use a pencil.' Someone people don't really like. Do you know anyone like that?"

Wilson patted Trevor on the back and shot him a devious smile. "Didn't you spray deodorant in Coach Fleming's face this morning?"

"Yeah."

"And didn't you indirectly cause the fire alarm sprinklers to go off in the cafeteria at lunch?"

Trevor nodded.

"Son, it looks like you've just found your answer."

Trevor Jones

By the drinking fountain
Pretty darn excited

1:44 p.m.

Why did it take me so long to see that the perfect candidate is ME?!

Now that I've made most of the seventh grade class mad at me, I'M the shoo-in to lose. Sure, it stinks that pretty much everyone hates me now, but at least I can help Libby. Silver lining!

More grayish than silver, but still sorta silver!

So I'll just mess up everything intentionally. I won't hang any posters or do any campaigning. And I'll say completely illogical stuff at the debate. There's NO WAY I can win!

Libby will reveal her amazing slogan, she'll win the election in a landslide, and then she'll be in a good mood for a whole YEAR. This plan may be one of my best ones yet.

Now all I have to do is tell Libby the good news.

* * *

"No, Trevor. I won't let you do this," Libby said as she nervously picked at her pencil eraser in Language Arts. The two whispered to each other in the back row while Mr. Lewis was busy counting copies of *Where the Red Fern Grows*.

"It's too late. I already completed all the necessary paperwork and gave it to Decker. And stop picking." Trevor snatched her pencil away. "As much as I don't want to admit it, your cousin was right—my popularity faded after just one incident. Or maybe two." He shook his head and added under his breath, "I mean, all I did was drop a soda bottle and spray some deodorant on the coach."

"That was *you*?"

He sighed. "I was popular for a while and now it's over. Whatever. But I'm the exact kind of loser you need to run against you for president. This will work." Trevor sat up straight and said the words with as much intensity as he could muster on such short notice. "I'll intentionally mess up at the debate when Mr. Everett asks the questions. I'll answer with something completely ridiculous, or change the subject and talk about how proud I am of our new No Deodorant Policy. It's going to work. I'm sure of it. Totally, almost completely sure of it. Which means there's *no way* I can win, and since your slogan is going to whup up on

Cindy's slogan, *you*, my friend, are going to be our next student class president."

"But Trevor, you hate doing things wrong. Or answering questions incorrectly. You can't even stand it if you write the wrong date on your paper. How are you ever going to be able to do this?"

It was obvious Libby was just trying to be nice, but there was no way Trevor could let his friend give up on her dream. If it meant figuring out a way to get over his problem of always answering questions correctly, well . . . he'd have to find the override button. He'd figure it out.

After all, this was something Libby had been destined for since birth. While Trevor's destiny—he felt—had pretty much been fulfilled *long* ago.

FOUND IN MS. JONES'S BABY SCRAPBOOK

"You need to be our student class president, Libby. And I'm going to help. Don't worry about it. This will work." He smiled at her, then noticed that Mr. Lewis had seemingly lost count and was starting over. At least they had more time to talk.

"One more thing!" Trevor added. "If I run against you, that means I can't be your manager."

"Oh, yeah?" Libby perked up at that. Where was he going with this?

"That means you're going to have to do it all on your own, I guess."

"Oh. All on my own."

"You can manage?" He winced.

Libby decided this was the time . . . the moment she should tell Trevor the truth about asking Molly to be her manager, too. But for some reason the words got stuck in her throat. The truth—that she thought he wouldn't be able to run a cool campaign—would crush him. Especially now that he'd mangled his popularity with most of the seventh grade. Not exactly the best time for your best friend to say soul-crushing stuff.

Libby dabbed at her forehead with the back of her hand. "Is it hot in here?"

"Not really. I asked about your manager—can you do it yourself?"

Libby looked straight ahead, wishing the truth would just come out. But it didn't. "Sure."

Trevor figured Libby was just saying this because she didn't want to hurt his feelings by "replacing" him. But she needed the help. How else was she going to get papers stapled, slogans written, and posters drawn?

At the end of class, as he reached for his backpack, he decided right then and there that he'd find her a campaign manager on his own . . . and he knew the perfect person. "You'll do fine, Libby. You'll win." Trevor smiled, then ran off down the hall.

There was someone he needed to find.

Trevor Jones

By his locker,
arms folded
contentedly

3:01 p.m.

I'm going to find Libby a new campaign manager.
She needs someone cool . . . someone with an attitude.
Someone different.

   She needs Molly Decker.

Libby Gardner

By her locker,
pacing, lots and
lots of it

3:02 p.m.

I should have told him that Molly is my manager.
Now he thinks I'm going to do all this myself.
And he's being such a great friend by offering to
run against us and volunteering to lose. Really,
sweetest thing ever.

What is wrong with me?!

I'll tell him. Today. This afternoon. I'll call
him tonight.

But right now, I really need to start figuring
out my campaign. I should take some deep, cleansing breaths. Find my happy, quiet place.

Because here's what's most important . . .
focusing on what it said on my onesie in my baby
picture: Born to Be Class President!

[takes deep, cleansing breath]

I can't let down my baby onesie.

CHAPTER TEN

AS STUDENTS FILLED THE HALLS TO HEAD HOME, THE intercom crackled yet again. "Students, I have one last announcement," Vice Principal Decker said, his voice sounding rather upbeat. "Good news! We will be able to hold the seventh grade presidential race after all since we now have a third candidate running: Trevor Jones!"

Throughout the hall, Trevor heard groans and even a few boos. He dropped his head, staring at his feet. Even though he was expecting this kind of reaction, it still stung. But at least it was obvious that his plan to run against Libby so he could lose was definitely going to work.

Trevor wished he could rush home and bring an end to

this humiliating day. But he couldn't—he still had prong one of Decker's punishment to deal with. So he hurried to the front office to call his mother for a ride home since he would miss the bus.

He wasn't looking forward to making this call, but at least it wasn't an *actual* detention, just some cafeteria duty. Which technically could end up being worse, Trevor feared, but anything sounded better than "detention."

After two rings, Ms. Jones picked up the phone.

"Mom, I'm not hurt." Trevor had learned long ago it was best to open an unexpected call with that line. It made any other news seem a lot less awful.

"That's good news," she said as she crunched down on an apple. "What's going on?"

"I spilled my soda on the floor at lunch, and some girls slipped in it and fell and screamed and the vice principal thought there was an emergency so he pulled the fire alarm, which made the sprinklers go off, and the cafeteria flooded, so now I have to stay after school and help the lunch lady. Mom? You still there?"

There was a pause on the line. Clearly, his mom needed a moment to take all of this in. Finally, Ms. Jones asked, "You mean you caused a group of girls to slip and fall?" It was a well-known fact that Trevor's mom was a big contributor to the Girl Power Fund of America (helping girls realize they *rock* since 1992!). Anything that went against the principles of Girl Power, like causing girls to slip on soda, was very upsetting to her.

"I didn't mean to—"

"Trevor, you know what this means?"

He hesitated. "No?" But he *did* know what it meant—lots of writing.

"Apology letters, Trevor. To each girl. Got it?"

"Yes, Mom."

"I'll pick you up in an hour. Have fun with the cafeteria lady."

When they hung up, Trevor let out a heavy sigh and looked up. That's when he saw Molly peeking at him around the office door. Or rather, staring.

She was walking by the office on her way to the bus when she noticed Trevor on the phone. She'd only heard part of his conversation, but she'd heard enough—Trevor was taking the blame for the incident in the cafeteria. Poor guy, she thought. Molly had been to plenty of schools and had seen this sort of thing before—sodas that spill, girls that fall, sprinklers that deploy. But usually nice guys like Trevor weren't to blame. She had a feeling this wasn't his fault at all.

She lowered her head and scuffled down the hall to catch her bus, wondering if there was a way to help him.

"Molly, wait up!" Trevor called after her. "I need your help." Molly wasn't exactly the type to hand out favors, so Trevor thought this might not work out. But he had to give it a shot.

People were pushing past them as they headed down the hallway, so Trevor quickly pulled her to the side and went on to explain how he planned to run against Libby and Cindy so that hopefully Libby would win.

"So how about if *you* take over as Libby's campaign manager?" he said. "But you can't tell her I asked you, because she'll think I don't believe in her, which makes her super moody and ends up getting my mother involved."

Molly calmly folded her arms. "Let me get this straight: You want me to be Libby's campaign manager but act like it was *my* idea, not yours. And you don't want me to tell Libby."

Trevor nodded energetically.

Molly couldn't believe she'd suddenly found herself in the middle of a full-on dramatic event. Both Trevor and Libby had asked her to be Libby's manager, but she wasn't supposed to tell either one of them? So peculiar! But it also made her feel pretty necessary. School at Westside was really starting to get bearable—not that she would admit that out loud.

FOUND SCRIBBLED ON THE
BOTTOM OF MOLLY'S SHOE

Today = :)

She stuck her hand out. "You have yourself a deal."

When Trevor entered the empty cafeteria, he fully expected to find a watery mess on the floor left over from the fire sprinkler, and that he'd be required to clean it all up. Which, if he were allowed to use Wilson's floor buffer, he really wouldn't mind one bit.

But over in the far corner, he noticed Wilson unplugging his floor buffer—he'd already cleaned the floor. Very shiny.

Wilson wrapped the cord around the machine and wheeled it over to Trevor as he whistled. "Looks pretty good, right?"

"Sorry you had to clean this yourself," Trevor said. "I was supposed to do that."

"Oh, no. You have plenty of other jobs to do here. But be on your toes." Wilson looked over at the lunch lady. "Jan's in a mood."

This worried Trevor. "The bad kind?"

Wilson shot the lunch lady a smile and said, "The best kind." He started whistling again and then he was gone.

Then why do I have to be on my toes? Trevor wondered.

"We're going to cook." Jan the lunch lady had suddenly appeared next to him. She was short and athletic with round glasses and hair cut in the shape of a mixing bowl. "It's not often that I get student help in the kitchen." She clasped her hands together as if student help were a very exciting concept. "Now, normally we cook in the morning, but since Vice Principal Decker said I'm supposed to make you appreciate the inner workings of a cafeteria—his words, not mine, dear—we're going to cook together this afternoon. Tomorrow is Terrific Creamed Spinach Tuesday. Isn't that exciting?!" Jan the lunch lady's eyes sparkled.

Perhaps this was what Wilson meant by the best kind of mood. Jan the lunch lady was in the mood to cook.

Trevor tried his hardest to break into a smile. "Exciting." Not a word he ever thought he would associate with creamed spinach. But Jan seemed eager.

She handed him an apron and a hairnet. "Put these on and come with me."

He hesitated. A *hairnet*? Reluctantly, Trevor followed her into the kitchen.

And his heart immediately dropped.

No, no. I can't do this, Trevor thought.

It wasn't that she'd asked him to cook. Or that she'd asked him to put on an apron and a hairnet. It was *where* he was supposed to wear these items while cooking Tuesday's terrific creamed spinach that was freaking him out. Though he had been coming to Westside for over a month now, he had never noticed that the buses dropped off and picked up right outside the cafeteria, or that there was an ENORMOUS floor-to-ceiling window in the cafeteria kitchen that overlooked the area.

Trevor cringed and turned to Jan the lunch lady. "So I'm supposed to make creamed spinach in front of a wall of windows overlooking the *entire* bus area while wearing a hairnet?"

"I do it all the time! The kids love peeking in the window to see what I'm cooking up. They'll be so excited to see that you're helping out." She pulled out a bag of spinach and nodded. "Okay, first we're going to boil the water. Then—"

"It's a wall. Of *windows*."

"Exactly!" Lunch Lady Jan was very excited.

There was no way out of this. Trevor was going to have to make creamed spinach while wearing a hairnet in front of practically the entire Westside student body. Talk about embarrassing. But his popularity had already been pulverized—what did a little more humiliation really matter? It didn't. Helping Libby win the election was really all that *did* matter at this point. And doing something humiliating would only increase his chances of losing.

He couldn't believe he was about to go through with this, all so he could help Libby win the election. But then again, she'd always had his back and he knew she'd do it for him.

So Trevor boldly stepped up to his pot of boiling water, dropped a huge handful of spinach into it, and stirred gently while ignoring the mocking glares from the crowd that had gathered outside.

Molly was out by the bus area and saw Trevor in the

window. She shook her head, feeling bad that this was the punishment her dad had given him. But she thought Trevor was pretty bold for going through with it. And truthfully, she also wished she could borrow that hairnet—she had a couple of ideas for ways she could sew it into an interesting accessory.

"Nice highlights. They're blue now." Corey Long had walked up next to her.

Molly rolled her eyes. "They've *always* been blue." She didn't understand why Corey would even talk to her. After she had turned down his invitation to go with him to the fall dance, she was amazed that he was constantly still trying to impress her. When would the guy understand it took *a lot* to impress her?

"What's everyone looking at?" Corey asked her.

Molly motioned to the cafeteria windows, where Trevor was being watched as if he were in a Macy's store display.

"You have *got* to be kidding. Trevor . . . cooking . . . in a hairnet?! This day keeps getting better!"

Molly looked Corey over and wondered why he was bent over laughing so hard. She grabbed him by the shoulder and pulled him back up. "Seriously. Why is this so funny to you?"

Corey took a moment to fix his hair, then answered,

giving her his best impressing-a-girl-with-blue-highlights smirk. "Get this. Today I shook Trevor's soda at lunch when he wasn't looking. And then in P.E. when he was in the bathroom, I rotated the nozzle on his deodorant. So radical, right?! I mean, ruining that guy's reputation has just been so easy. And now he's . . . now . . . the hairnet . . ." Corey bent over and went back to belly laughing. "Can't . . . breathe . . ."

Molly couldn't believe what she was hearing. *Corey* did all that? She stepped up to him and crossed her arms tightly. "*You're* the one who should be wearing that hairnet, Corey. And when Trevor finds out, he'll stand up to you."

"*That* kid?" Corey pointed to Trevor, who was now letting Lunch Lady Jan taste test the creamed spinach. "He'd never stand up to me. He's the one who's making it so easy for me to ruin his reputation."

Corey started belly laughing again. Molly watched as Trevor stirred his pot of creamed spinach, and she caught his eye. He waved at her with his spatula, bits of spinach sliding down and splashing into the pot. The students watching laughed at him, but Trevor just smiled and kept waving.

Molly wondered if maybe he'd actually remembered

what she'd said earlier about the definition of cool: *Do it anyway, because you don't care what people think.* Impressive, she thought.

Molly poked Corey on the shoulder. "Hey. I don't know why you even told me all this. You don't impress me." Then she added under her breath, "Someone else does."

Just then, Corey pulled himself together and stood up straight. "What do you mean?" he asked her.

Molly clenched her jaw—Corey was the *last* person she was going to explain herself to.

Instead, she turned and stormed off.

Trevor Jones

Standing in front
of his mom's
station wagon

Still wearing a
hairnet

3:55 p.m.

I have no clue what that was about, but Molly sure looked steamed at Corey. And then did you see how she stormed off? Pretty cool, actually.

Anyway.

That storming-off thing? It made me realize . . . I have to talk to Libby. She needs to know that I asked Molly to be her campaign manager. I wouldn't ever want her mad at me—you know, storming off and stuff. The last thing I want is for her to think I asked Molly to replace me because I didn't think Libby could do this on her own. Which is true, actually, but I don't want her to THINK that. It's a rude thought, so I guess sometimes the truth is rude.

I'll break it to her gently. Over the phone. Today. This afternoon. I'll call her tonight.

WESTSIDE
MIDDLE SCHOOL

THAT
NIGHT

CHAPTEя
ELEVEN

LIBBY HAD TO MAKE THE CALL. **S**HE PACED HER BEDROOM floor going over exactly what she would say to Trevor. The perfect words. The tone. Whether she should get right to it or ease into the subject slowly. Maybe getting to it sooner rather than later would be the best way, like getting chores done before playing.

There was a lot to think about before dialing his number.

But she didn't have to think for long, because at that very moment, the phone rang. Looking at the caller ID, she let out a little gasp. It was Trevor.

"Just wanted to tell you something real quick," Trevor said without even saying hello. He had rehearsed exactly what he was going to say and he'd decided that if he said it "real quick" it would be less painful, like ripping off a Band-Aid.

"What is it?" she asked, wondering how long this was going to take, because she figured maybe it would be best to go ahead and get to her giant, scary topic right away.

Trevor cleared his throat. "Here's the thing. I know you can run your campaign by yourself, but everyone needs help from time to time—even the U.S. president has a campaign manager."

Libby was excited to hear that he was talking about the same topic she wanted to talk about. "Oh! So you're thinking . . ."

Trevor sensed she really wanted him to get to the point. *Rip the Band-Aid off.* Then he blurted it out all at once. "I asked Molly to be your campaign manager because she's different and cool and dark and it's okay to need help and don't be mad and are you mad?"

"You asked Molly to be my manager?"

"Don't be mad." He flinched, then felt ridiculous, as if that would help him escape an arm punch through the phone.

Libby paused, taking a moment to consider this news. If Trevor had asked Molly to be her manager, then there was really no reason to tell him that *she* had already asked

Molly earlier that day. Besides, Trevor had just had the world's worst day on record. Numerous people on the bus had told her that they'd seen him cooking cafeteria food while wearing a hairnet. She wasn't about to bring any more pain to his day. She could just agree to this, and no feelings would get hurt. Boom, done. They could move on.

"I'm not mad," she announced. "It's a good idea. I'll let Molly be my manager. She probably has some good ideas that are different from Cindy's, and she could be helpful. Thanks, Trevor."

Thanks? He didn't expect that. More like some huffing and stomping and then hopefully some slow acceptance. So this was shocking.

"Oh. Um . . . Right. Okay. So . . . this is great, right?! Molly will be your new manager. You should give her a call tonight."

"I will, Trev."

"And tomorrow we'll start campaigning. You will be awesome . . . I will be horrible."

Libby giggled. A nervous giggle. "Best plan ever."

The next morning, Libby, Trevor, and Molly met in the school lobby before homeroom for a campaign planning meeting.

Since Trevor wasn't actually campaigning, his poster was just a big white space with VOTE FOR TREVOR written in very small letters in the middle. He had to at least *pretend* he was running. He left the two of them alone and headed down the hall to put up his one poster.

Molly turned to Libby and raised a brow. "Well? Did you write up a bio like I told you last night?"

"And I stapled it, too," Libby said, trying to stand a little taller. "Just like you asked, since you said you don't do any work that involves office supplies."

"Just not the boring office supplies. I'd use a laminating machine." Molly then narrowed her eyes. "So. Did you dig far into your past? Pull up the rich history of who you are? The deep stuff. We need to know the *real* you."

Libby handed over the two-page document. "It's all in there. Super deep."

Molly took a moment to look it over, then shook her head. "Deep? This is all about earning a Girl Scouts Brownie Citizen badge in third grade."

"That badge was hard fought. The little seedling I planted took months of nurturing to grow. It's still only a foot-and-a-half tall now, but the sweat that I shed for that little tree was worth it."

Molly puffed out her cheeks and stared at the ceiling.

Finally she looked straight at Libby and calmly said, "Maybe we should just start with a slogan instead."

The buses had arrived, and students began to fill the halls to get to their classes. Just then, Cindy bounced up and snatched the papers out of Molly's hand. "A two-page bio? Wow!" she said with sarcasm in her voice.

Molly liked to fight sarcasm with sarcasm. She narrowed her eyes as she examined Cindy's shirt. "Nice button. And such a catchy slogan."

Cindy looked down at her button—which said VOTE FOR CINDY!—then back up at Molly. "Thanks! Do you notice there's a second *smaller* button on it? Push it."

"I don't push things."

"Oh, you should push it."

This was sounding like a dare to Molly. She did not like dares. Though she often took them.

Libby held her hand out to stop Molly, but it was too late. Cindy had pushed Molly's button figuratively, so Molly pushed Cindy's button literally. But after Molly pushed the button, she was, well . . . shocked. Apparently, there had been many technological advances made in the field of cute button making.

"Totally cute, right?! See ya!" Cindy bounced off, leaving Libby's bio on the floor behind her.

Molly turned to Libby. "Her button just poofed glitter *in my face.*"

"Need a tissue?"

Molly ignored her and wiped the glitter off as best she could. Then she said, "We have to beat her."

"Yep. That, too." Libby pulled her sleeve down and

dabbed at Molly's cheek to get more of the glitter off, though she wasn't very successful.

"She's a girl who thinks she can get votes with glitter and buttons and poof," Molly said between dabs. "But *you're* the one who made flyers with *information*. We need to go in the opposite direction."

Libby nodded in agreement. "Be different."

Molly stepped away from Libby and paced the hall. "Not cute. Not glittery. Not poofy . . . opposite."

Libby paced alongside her. "We're going opposite!"

"That's right!" Molly narrowed her eyes. "We're going to go dark. Rude. NEGATIVE."

Libby came to a halt. "Negative?!" She bit at her lip. Certainly she didn't mind being different—being different was always cool (except in cases of shoe wear and such). But going *negative*? She didn't want to regret winning because of *how* she won. Except here she was with only two days left before the debate, without pamphlets, posters, slogans . . . nothing. While Cindy Applegate had a whole campaign figured out and an entire team behind her.

Maybe Molly was her only hope.

With a sneaky smirk, Molly leaned in and said, "I know . . . let's go werewolf on her."

Libby dropped her shoulders. She really didn't see any

other choice but to follow Molly's lead. So she answered, her voice weak, "Werewolf. Sounds great, Molly."

From down the hall, Trevor watched Libby's shoulders drop—he'd recognize that movement anywhere . . . the sure sign of disappointment. What was going on?

He quickly approached them and noticed that Molly's face was strangely sparkly. "What happened to you?" he asked her. "Did you fall on top of an art project?"

"It was Cindy Applegate's button." Molly folded her arms and flicked her eyes back and forth between Libby and Trevor. "Look, if Libby's going to win this, she's going to have to go in the opposite direction of glittery."

"That's right," Libby said to Trevor with a shaky smile. "Nothing poofy. Nothing cute. I'm sure I'll come up with something dark and rude soon." And then she dropped her shoulders again.

Corey Long

Pacing the hall,
looking slightly
worried

8:29 a.m.

So that Molly with the blue hair told me that Libby really needs to win the election. TREVOR is the third person running against her and Cindy with the gum. Which is strange because I thought Trevor was her friend or something.

[paces nervously]

And I mean, I know Libby hates me now and all. And she has every right to—taking her to that dance just to get algebra answers wasn't the coolest of moves, I guess.

But if we ever had another dance—I know she wouldn't believe this—I'd ask her to go with me. For real this time. She's pretty cool. Or at least, I need to find out if she's cool. I have a feeling she might be.

So I figured since I ruined the dance for Libby, helping her win the election will make her see I'm not such a bad guy. In fact, I'm actually the good guy, pretty much and stuff.

I'm like Batman in that movie *Batman*.

[leans in closer, adjusts hair strands]

And she's been smiling lately. Well, this one time she did. I think at ME. But I could be wrong . . . so I'm not about to let Trevor win student class president and give her ANY reason to wipe that smile off her face. I can fix this.

I'm Batman.

CHAPTER TWELVE

CAMPAIGNING CONTINUED THROUGHOUT THE MORNING. Libby and Molly would meet between classes to discuss possible slogans, but they couldn't reach an agreement. Libby was not okay with Molly's top suggestion: VOTE FOR LIBBY, BECAUSE CINDY DOESN'T EVEN KNOW WHICH SIDE OF TOWN WESTSIDE IS LOCATED IN.

"But we don't know Cindy doesn't know that," Libby argued.

"Doesn't matter. By the time she's done defending her sense of direction, the election is over. That's the beauty of a negative campaign."

But in the end, Libby simply couldn't attack Cindy's sense of direction (or lack thereof). It seemed so mean. This going negative thing was going to be difficult for her.

Meanwhile, Trevor continued campaigning by not campaigning. His one poster was enough—no need for flyers. And he certainly wasn't going to talk to anyone about his campaign, especially since he didn't have one. So he spent the time in between classes hanging out by his locker.

As he was gathering his books for science, he saw Cindy and her Team Cindy! entourage, which had now multiplied to a group of at least ten, coming down the hall. They oozed through the crowd in the hallway like a peppy pink blob. Trevor pressed his back against his locker, hoping he wouldn't get sucked in as they passed by.

When they did, he noticed they all wore the exact same T-shirt, yet again.

Trevor found it weird that Cindy had a T-shirt for every occasion—even the Hallmark card company wasn't this dedicated. But he had to admit that her shirts were helping him keep track of time.

Because if the debate was in two days, Libby needed to get serious *now*. The two of them had been friends since birth, so he knew she needed a good forty-eight hours to get prepared for something this big.

He spotted her by her locker and headed toward her, but he was stopped when a large foot landed in front of him, blocking his path. "I hear you're running for student class president."

Trevor's eyes lifted and met Corey's. He needed to react quickly. Turn and run? Scream for help? Fake an allergy attack and call for the nurse? But he decided he was done with those options, and maybe the best way out was to be straightforward. No emotion—just the truth. "Yes."

"You're never going to win."

"I know."

Corey poked him on the shoulder. "Seriously. You're going to lose."

"Absolutely." Wow, Trevor thought. Telling the truth without emotion is pretty easy.

"I don't think you're hearing me right. If you run for

student class president"—Corey leaned in and squinted at him—"you . . . will . . . lose."

Trevor nodded. "There's no doubt about it. Bye." He walked off toward Libby. Before he reached her locker, he looked back at Corey, who was scratching his head and looking very confused.

What was THAT all about? Corey wondered. That dude can't talk to me like that. He's gonna regret it.

Trevor's day continued along without incident. He was even starting to feel unnoticed (in a good way). It was only one day into his new life as the regular old Trevor, and he was almost comfortable again. He no longer had to worry about finger and palm placement when high-fiving. There weren't all those frantic moments of having to say the perfect words in the right order just to uphold his impeccable reputation.

He hadn't spilled anything, broken anything, ruined anyone's life—particularly not his own—in almost three hours. Trevor felt downright relaxed. It wasn't as if his actions could cause him to be any more detested than he already was.

But in science class, the intercom crackled. Just the click of that intercom caused him to flinch. Because lately, every announcement seemed to involve something about him.

"Students," Vice Principal Decker announced, "you might have noticed that there is a very strange smell slowly spreading throughout the entire school."

Just as he said the words, it happened. The smell wafted into their classroom—a horrible stench that was a mixture of old tires and rotten fish and moldy bread.

"Ewww!" a bunch of students responded as they pinched their noses.

"Apparently, when the air-conditioning clicked on early this morning, the smell was carried through the ventilation system, and now . . ." Decker hesitated before delivering the worst of the news. "Well, we're finding it *very* difficult to determine the source."

Whew! Trevor sat back in his seat, feeling relaxed. Finally an announcement from Vice Principal Decker that had nothing to do with him. There was no way he could have caused this horrible smell.

But when he looked up, all eyes were on him. His stomach dropped. Since most ridiculous incidents lately could be traced back to him, it made sense, really, that his classmates would assume that he was somehow at fault. *Not this time!* he wanted to yell.

Just then, one of the Baker twins tapped on his shoulder and pointed toward the hall. Standing there was Corey Long, holding his nose and pointing at him. *Huh?*

Trevor figured Libby was right—there was no way a guy like Corey was simply going to forget about being drenched with orange soda in front of the entire school at a dance. There was going to be payback someway.

But seriously? Trevor thought. A bad smell in the ventilation system? What a weirdo.

"So to get to the bottom of this," Vice Principal Decker continued, "we have called in some experts who specialize in hazardous materials. Wilson will be in charge of escorting them around the school to locate the source of the smell. We ask that you leave the men in hazmat suits alone and let them do their job. Do not be scared of them—they look intimidating, but that's because they're experts. The suits are just a precaution; no need to be concerned. But if any of you comes across anything suspicious, please tell me. Again . . . do not be afraid."

A wave of worried rumbles spread through the class as the students reacted to the news. Their school was about to be taken over by a team of highly trained specialized experts in the field of hazardous materials. The students weren't afraid . . . they were *petrified*. And they blamed Trevor.

Corey Long

Peeking around a
hallway corner
to get a better
view of the
hazmat crew

2:21 p.m.

Those hazmat guys are AWESOME! But naw, I didn't actually cause that smell. I have NO IDEA where that stench is coming from. I mean . . . that's just gross, dude!

But that doesn't mean I'm not going to take this perfect opportunity to peg it on Trevor! Everyone will believe me, so why not?

It's like that movie *Robin Hood*, where I'm taking from the rich and giving to the poor. Only it's cool kids and nerdy kids.

Only that doesn't make sense.

Okay, so it's probably more of a Superman thing, because Superman is always cool no matter what.

I'm Superman.

Wilson

Looking quite
unimpressed

2:25 p.m.

This is completely unnecessary. My janitorial training has provided me with the skills to handle tracking down an unknown smell.

I know every inch of this school backward and forward, inside and out. The ventilation ducts, the piping, the wiring, the teachers' mailboxes—all of it.

But what those so-called "scientists" don't understand is they won't find the source of that smell by tracing it through the air ducts.

No sirree.

It's the students. You have to study the students' behavior. THAT'S how you'll find your answer.

They'll give themselves away. . . . They always do.

CHAPTER THIRTEEN

THAT EVENING, TREVOR WENT OVER TO LIBBY'S HOUSE to check on her debate preparation. Even though Molly was her campaign manager and technically that was her job, he still held the title of best friend. She might need someone to alphabetize her pamphlets or help arrange her visual aids. He was guessing she'd made a pull-down retractable wall chart with her slogan. Things that retracted were her favorite.

Mrs. Gardner answered the door with a frazzled look on her face, but it turned to a look of relief when she saw Trevor standing there. When she led him to Libby's bedroom, Trevor understood why. Scattered around the room were empty bottles of ranch dressing, bowls of Starbursts, and tangled webs of yarn. At least the Starbursts were separated by color—this attempt at organization was a start. A start toward *what,* he had no idea.

"Need anything, honey?" Mrs. Gardner asked, looking around the filthy room. "Cleaning supplies, maybe?"

Libby shook her head without making eye contact.

So Trevor stepped over some nests of yarn and said to Mrs. Gardner, "I'll help get this straightened up, Mrs. G. Where's the trash can?"

"Thanks, Trevor. You're a good friend." Then she pointed across the room to the almost-filled trash can in the corner.

Trevor noticed that Libby's campaign posters were still in there—the ones she'd thrown away when her cousin Luke had laughed at them.

Those don't belong in the trash, he thought.

Mrs. Gardner left the two of them, and Trevor took a moment to look over the mess. "Sooo . . . Lib? What's up with the yarn and Starbursts?" he asked as he wandered around gathering trash.

"If I come up with a reasonable slogan, I treat myself with a reward. An A idea earns me a red Starburst. For B ideas I get to eat an orange, and so on all the way down to the F ideas."

"What color goes with those?"

"Yellow."

"How many of those have you eaten?"

"Lost count. They're already gone."

"You haven't lost your mind, have you? Maybe eating so many yellow Starbursts isn't a good idea?"

"Nope. This yarn-and-Starburst brainstorming technique will definitely work. I've never been more organized!" she yelped as she twirled strands of frayed hair around her finger.

"So then, what's the yarn for?" He glared down at a tangled web of unused yarn.

She crinkled her nose. "I have no idea."

FOUND IN TREVOR'S NOTEBOOK

No more yellow Starbursts for this girl.

Trevor narrowed his eyes. "I'm guessing you haven't come up with a slogan yet."

She flopped down on her bed. "Nope."

Trevor felt helpless—maybe Libby had listened too closely to Cousin Luke's advice about middle school campaigns needing to be cool. After all, the girl was in her bedroom surrounded by candy wrappers and a tangled web of yarn without a campaign platform two nights before the students were to vote. This wasn't the Libby he knew.

Trevor wasn't her manager anymore, but he had to do *something*.

"Let's try to do the pencil-and-paper thing and come up with some ideas," he said.

She tilted her head. "No color coding with yarn and Starbursts?"

He patted the top of her hand. "Let's take a break from that for now. First tell me what your best slogan has been so far."

She hesitated, not wanting to share just how bad her best slogan was. "Vote for Libby. She's giddy," she finally mumbled.

He started to write the words, then stopped and erased them. "You know, we don't have to write down *every* idea.

Let's just focus on the issues you want the campaign to be about." The thought of Corey threatening to stop him from winning the election came to Trevor's mind. "Maybe bullying?"

Libby nodded and rubbed her hands together. "How about 'Stop being mean, it's not nice, there are other ways to express your anger, perhaps there are issues with your siblings—'"

"Libby, that's not a slogan. That's an afternoon talk show. Are you okay?"

She covered her face with her hands. "I can't do this!"

"Of course you can. You were *born* to do this."

Libby looked up at him, her eyes slightly red. "Not anymore, Trevor. This stuff has always come easy to me, but for the first time in my life I can't figure it out. Not even with all the organization and yarn and Starbursts in the world. Maybe it's a sign. Cindy is going to win."

Trevor didn't understand what was going on. Running campaigns *had* always been so easy for Libby. True, the dry-erase marker campaign of sixth grade didn't land her a victory, but it was the best anti–dry-erase marker speech he'd ever heard. Where was *that* girl?

"But you did so great with your speech last year. What's going on, Libby?"

She pushed off her bed and sat on the floor. From under the corner of her bed, she noticed it peeking out—her shoe box of old notes. That's when the memories flooded in. And the contents of that box.

It hit her exactly why this was all so hard for her now.

LIBBY'S SHOE BOX OF NOTES

Libby pulled the box out and placed it in her lap. "Remember two summers ago when Jessica Lymon moved in to that old house on the corner?"

"The girl who always wore sunglasses. Sure, I remember."

"And the platform flip-flops and designer cutoff jean shorts—" Libby added.

"You followed her around that entire summer."

Libby propped her elbow on her knee and rested her head on her hand. "I'd never met anyone like her. Jessica knew everything about fashion and decorating. And her parents came in and ripped up that old house and refurbished it. I spent that whole summer learning about postmodernist architecture and sustainable green homes. We'd sit on her front lawn and flip through magazines, looking at pictures of granite countertops and solar panels. Even these organizational bins under my bed were her idea. They're made from recycled plastic." Libby took a deep breath, then added in a soft voice, "Jessica was the definition of cool. And I couldn't believe she wanted to be friends with me."

Trevor folded his arms. "I remember, Lib. But I never liked that girl. She thought she was *better* than you."

"Let's face it," Libby said. "She *was* better than me." She lifted up the top of the box and pulled out a worn piece of paper. "But at the end of the summer, when they moved to go renovate another house, I decided to write Jessica a good-bye note. I wrote it on my Hola! Kitty Cat! sketch paper because I thought maybe she'd think it was cute." Libby shook her head, not wanting to recall the rest. "But I guess because it wasn't written on recycled bamboo leaf paper or something, she took one look at it and laughed."

"She laughed?"

"Not in a good way." Libby opened the note, her hands slightly trembling, so Trevor could see. "She wrote this on it and handed it back. I never heard from her again." Libby dipped her head and a tear dropped to the floor. "I'm not cool, Trevor. I don't think I ever will be."

Trevor couldn't believe someone like Jessica Lymon could think she knew everything there was to know about being cool just because of her clothes and her recycled countertops. And he decided right then and there, if there was one thing that needed to be thrown in the trash, it was that note.

Trevor crouched down next to her. "But you have a secret weapon."

Libby flicked her eyes up at him. "I do?"

"Molly. She's your campaign manager now. She gave you good advice, right?"

"To be dark. And negative." Libby shook her head. "That's *her* strength, not mine."

Trevor wasn't sure what to say. She needed a pep talk, but that would require lots of pep and lots of talk. The right kind, too. And he wasn't sure he could figure it out.

But he had to at least try.

"You're going to win—I am going to lose on purpose. And Cindy's going to lose because of glitter." He wasn't really sure what else to say, so he unwrapped a red Starburst and placed it in her hand. "There's nothing to worry about."

Trevor Jones

Outside Libby's
house, chewing on
two red Starbursts

5:52 p.m.

There's a LOT to worry about. In all my twelve years as Libby's professional best friend, I've NEVER seen her like this.

Except that one time she got a little strange when the store ran out of her favorite containers. But that doesn't come close to this.

And now I'm pretty sure Corey Long is trying to get revenge by blaming me for the horrible smell that even those scientists in bunny suits can't find. How am I going to fix that?! I'm under a lot of pressure here.

This type of thing is usually the perfect job for Libby . . . you know . . . the fixing of my life, and all. But clearly, she's in no condition to fix anything right now. And that was supposed to be a pep talk I just gave her, but it didn't seem to do much good.

Man, I really wish eating red Starbursts could solve problems—I've already eaten six.

CHAPTER FOURTEEN

MOLLY ARRIVED AT SCHOOL EARLY WITH ROLLED-UP posters under her arm. The night before, she'd received a frantic call from Libby, but she couldn't quite understand everything Libby was saying. Something about ideas and Starbursts and a note from some girl named Jessica. But what Molly *could* make sense of was that Libby still hadn't come up with a cool slogan, so it was going to have to be up to her.

Molly stood at the entrance of the school and watched Libby quickly get out of her mother's car.

Libby rushed inside, looking as if her hair hadn't met up with a hairbrush in quite some time. "You did it for me? Finished the posters?"

"Worked all night on them."

Libby stuck her hands on her hips. "You didn't go *super* negative or anything. Right?"

"This is middle school. Get your head in the game." She unrolled one of the posters and proudly showed it to her.

"Molly! We can't use that!"

"Of course we can. And we're going to win with this. It's unexpected. It's cool."

But the word *whatever* zinged around in Libby's brain—the same word Jessica Lymon had used in her cruel note. For some reason that word hurt almost just as much as being told she wasn't cool. It meant she didn't care.

Libby shivered inside a little. "You're going to give me nightmares with this poster. Roll it up. We'll start over with something else."

Just then, Trevor entered the front door—he'd also asked his mom for a early ride to school so he could help Libby with campaign prep if she needed it. But he was shocked when he heard Libby's and Molly's very loud voices.

"The debate is tomorrow, Libby. You're the one who wanted my help. But now I'm starting to think you *want* to lose!"

"What?!" Libby yelped.

This increase in volume caused the students in the hallway to turn and see what was going on. Trevor hurried over to them. "What's wrong?"

"Libby doesn't want my help."

"Molly went werewolf!"

"Wait, wait, slow down. And lower your voices before you get in trouble."

Libby stepped closer to Trevor. "I told Molly she could go dark, but I didn't mean pitch-black. And there's no way I can use her poster."

"Forget it, Libby! You knew exactly what you were getting when you asked me to be your manager."

Trevor nodded. "She has a point. When you asked her . . . Wait . . . When *you* asked *her* to be your manager?"

Molly folded her arms. "Yep, Libby came to *me* to be her manager—that's what our lunch meeting was about." She shoved the poster into Libby's hands. "Here. Do it on your own now—just like you told Trevor you could."

As Molly strutted off, Libby dropped her head.

This information was not what Trevor was expecting. He slowly turned to her. "You asked Molly to be your manager? You were planning on replacing me?"

Libby sighed deeply. It was time to tell Trevor exactly why she had asked Molly. He deserved the truth. "Not replacing, really. I asked Molly because I needed her to be devious and . . . cool. No offense, Trev, but you were cool for almost an entire week, and that's great and all, but then it disappeared like a rub-on tattoo. Just like my cousin Luke said it would."

Trevor couldn't believe he was hearing this. She chose

Molly over him because she'd help run a cooler campaign? Had Libby forgotten about the friends-since-birth part?!

"So you only trusted me with stapling papers, but Molly was the one who got to come up with cool campaign slogans." His face reddened. Under his breath he added, "After everything I've done . . . you went behind my back? You figured I'd mess everything up."

"It's not like that."

"It *is* like that. And now you expect me to get up in front of the entire school and lose this election on purpose? And look like a fool—just for you?"

"I never expected you to. Trevor, you don't have to do this."

After the previous night's pep talk and years of being her campaign manager and a lifetime of friendship, Trevor couldn't believe it had suddenly come to this. Her going behind his back, not believing in him, not caring that he was about to humiliate himself in front of the entire student body on purpose. He simply couldn't let this happen.

Time for a change of plans.

"You're right, Libby. I *don't* have to get up there and make a fool of myself."

Libby drew her eyebrows together. "What do you mean? You're dropping out of the race?"

"No, I'm still going to run. But now I'm going to *win*." He spun on his heel and stormed off.

Cindy Applegate

Outside the girls'
bathroom(also
known as Gossip
Central)

8:27 a.m.

Whoa. GET. THIS.

So I heard from this girl Amanda who heard from this girl Becca with Braces that Libby and Molly were fighting in the hallway. I'm not sure if that meant they were just arguing, you know VERBALLY? Or if they were ATTACKING each other with their hands and stuff, but I'm guessing someone got hurt and had to go to the nurse for an ice pack.

That's not spreading gossip, that's just making an educated guess—something I learned about in science class. And since I'm trying to get better about not spreading gossip, I'm now proud of myself for using the scientific process ALL THE TIME.

Trevor Jones

Standing where
the soda machine
used to be

8:28 a.m.

I had to do it. There's no way I can let my already pummeled reputation get smooshed into tiny . . . bits of . . . grainy sand . . . molecule bits. Or something. My point is THIS: it's time for me to take matters into my own hands, since Libby clearly isn't worried about how this might hurt me.

So there. I'm going to do what it takes to win the election.

And that means I need a campaign manager, quick. Probably not a good idea to hire Molly, since she's in a pretty bad mood now. But I still need someone who can think differently.

[taps chin]

And I think I know just the person.

CHAPTER FIFTEEN

"**M**ARTY! WAIT UP!" TREVOR CAUGHT UP WITH Marty, who was reading a magazine as he lingered outside his homeroom class just before the bell rang. "I need a favor from you."

Marty looked up from his article in *Extreme Hunter* magazine. "Trevor, did you know the leading cause of death for blue jays is car accidents?"

"That's horrible, Marty, and I don't think that's accurate, but I—"

"Says here on page fifty-seven that if the public just knew these statistics that—"

"Yep, I'm sure the public would be outraged. Listen, right now, though, I don't need blue jay awareness help; I need regular help."

Marty lifted a brow. "Like what?"

"I need you to run my campaign for student class president. You need to be my manager, Marty. You're an eighth grader—you're smarter and bigger and you know what page to turn to in an emergency."

Marty nodded in agreement because all of that was really true.

"But the most important part?" Trevor clamped down on Marty's shoulder to make sure he was listening. "It needs to be cool. Like *really* cool. I need a cool slogan, cool platform, cool everything. Can you do that?"

Of course he could. He was an eighth grader. Marty had been through all the pitfalls of seventh grade, which included being locked in the janitor's closet, and he'd survived. So running a cool campaign was not a problem. "Not a problem, Trevor."

"Great. But the vote is tomorrow."

"This is a problem."

"Why? I realize we'll have to do some quick campaigning, but surely we can—"

Marty paced nervously. "These things take time. We need focus groups. An action plan. You can't just throw a campaign together during a five-minute hallway conversation."

Across the hall, Cindy and her ever-growing peppy blob of supporters were putting up posters on the wall.

Trevor motioned to the poster and said to Marty, "If we don't pull a campaign together, Cindy Applegate might become our next class president. And I know you're going out with her, but I'm pretty sure she'd change the official school color to *glitter*."

Marty tightened his jaw and said softly, "I'm not going out with her. She broke up with me. She wants to keep her options open, or something like that."

After a long moment of staring at Cindy and her friends as they decorated the wall, Marty finally turned to Trevor. "Fine. Get a blank poster and a pen. Let's do this."

Throughout the day, Marty and Trevor joined up during passing periods and at lunchtime to discuss strategy, prepare for the following day's debate, and put up the posters Marty had made.

Marty walked and talked as he explained his strategy. "We'll plaster flyers on bathroom doors and we can make coffee mugs and water bottles and key chains and little magnets—"

"Look, the debate is tomorrow and then we vote. We should keep it simple."

Marty came to a stop. "Actually, we probably need to deal with our biggest issue first."

"Issue?"

"Stinkgate. The smell that's wafting through the

school—it doesn't bother me because I'm used to smelling dead carcasses from hunting. But the rest of the kids here think that you had something to do with it."

"Maybe the smell is just coming from all of the seventh grade boys not wearing deodorant?"

Marty took a whiff of air. "No. Definitely NOT body odor. It's something else. Trust me, page forty-two of last year's March issue of *Boys' Life* teaches you how to tell the differences between offensive smells. It's not a skunk or sulfur or a hidden Easter egg that was never found"—Marty lifted a brow—"which is more common than you'd think."

"But why me? Just because I sprayed Coach Fleming with deodorant? And caused the sprinkler to go off in the cafeteria?"

"Reputations and rumors. They're hard to shake."

They were interrupted when three hazmat crew members rounded the corner. All the students pressed their backs up against the wall to let them by.

Trevor swallowed hard. Once they were gone, he grabbed Marty by the shoulders. "Help me. Show them that I had nothing to do with this."

Marty narrowed his eyes and thought it over. "It'll take some damage control. But I think I can spin this—I can turn your image around. Two words: lots of free beef jerky." He clamped down on Trevor's shoulder. "I think I smell victory."

Marty Nelson

Waiting for the
bus after school,
pencil tucked
behind his ear

2:35 p.m.

Don't tell Trevor, but I put together a focus group. I don't want to tell him because he's all freaked out that we don't have time for all this election prep. When actually, all I did was talk to some kids as they passed by my locker in between classes. Anyway.

Apparently, the average seventh grade voter feels Trevor is too conservative on the topic of P.E. equipment replacement. We'll have to work on that.

They also still feel he's cool for that orange soda incident that happened with Corey Long—so that's good. But some of them also feel Trevor is too short. Which wasn't even a question, so I don't know how that one came up.

Oh, and ALL of them feel he's responsible for the strange smell through the school.

So the debate is going to be crucial for him. It's a good thing he has my help.

WESTSIDE
MIDDLE SCHOOL
DEBATE
DAY

CHAPTER SIXTEEN

TODAY WAS THE DAY—DEBATE DAY—AND TREVOR HAD come prepared. Last night, Marty had come over, and they had researched what the standard questions were for a student council debate. They had shared a bag of barbecue-flavored turkey jerky and practiced his answers over and over.

While Trevor was ready for the debate, he *wasn't* ready for how he felt when he saw Libby at the bus stop that morning—he felt deserted. She stood a minimum of six kids away at all times and sat on the opposite end of the bus from him. No words, no eye contact, not even a hair flip in his direction.

How dare she give me the silent treatment! I should be giving HER the silent treatment.

And that's exactly what he did. The entire way to school, Trevor didn't look at her or talk to her, just turned to full-on silent treatment mode.

At the beginning of homeroom, Mr. Everett motioned for Trevor to come up to his desk. Trevor scuffled to the front of the room.

"Yes, Mr. Everett?" He stuffed his hands in his pockets. "Did you have a question?"

Mr. Everett waved a paper in Trevor's face. "This. It's a note from Counselor Plimp. She's requested a meeting with you. Apparently, she's worried about your behavior lately and needs to discuss this with you."

"My behavior?"

Mr. Everett casually sipped his tea. "You know . . . with you causing all these new rule changes at Westside, and things getting sort of strange around here . . ." He glanced over at some students who had covered their noses with makeshift masks—the unidentified smell in the school had gotten *that* bad. Trevor had somehow gotten used to it already, but he was certain he did not cause this smell. *Completely* certain. Or maybe more like *fairly* certain, if he was pressed about it in a court of law or something.

"Head on down to her office."

Trevor started to turn to leave, but Mr. Everett tilted

his glasses down and added one more thing. "Is there . . . Is everything okay, Trevor?"

Trevor considered his question. *Was* everything okay? No, it really wasn't. He'd tried his best to help Libby win student class president, but then she went behind his back, and everything fell apart. Now he had to find some way to win the election, salvage his reputation, and get back at Libby. Not exactly his idea of a fun afternoon.

Because, no matter what, it all resulted in him and Libby now giving each other the silent treatment. And meanwhile, Mr. Everett was still waiting for an answer to his question: Was everything okay?

The first thing that came to mind was something profound yet sort of sassy that his Mystical 7 Ball had once told him. "Nope," he said.

As if he understood, Mr. Everett simply nodded at Trevor, handed him a hall pass, and sent him on his way.

As Trevor walked in to Miss Plimp's waiting room, he was greeted by the pleasant smell of gardenias. (Somehow, the foul odor permeating the halls had not found its way into the guidance counselor's office.) The room was full of comfy plush chairs and the walls were painted a happy color—something in the peach family. Trevor couldn't help feeling a little bit calmer, maybe even almost relaxed. Miss Plimp had her back to him and was straightening posters on the wall.

"Uh, hi, Miss Plimp. Mr. Everett said you wanted to see me?"

Miss Plimp turned and smiled widely, and she clapped her hands three times, as if something big were about to start. "Hello, Trevor! Yes, I did want to see you. Why don't you go ahead and wait for me in my office—I'll be in there in just a minute!"

Miss Plimp sounded like a grown-up cheerleader.

Trevor assumed this was a requirement for the job. Every school counselor he'd ever come across had excessive perk. And when he entered Miss Plimp's office, he encountered even *more*. Except it was in the form of wide-eyed kittens.

She had stuffed animal kittens, porcelain kittens, kitten calendars, a famous paw print of Morris the Cat, and even a mounted hair ball that must have had some significance to her, but Trevor decided he wouldn't ask.

He'd never seen someone with quite this much dedication to cat culture. A section of her bookshelf was even labeled "Feline Fiction."

But then a poster hanging behind her desk caught his eye.

Trevor wasn't sure if he was supposed to be motivated to HANG IN THERE or develop a fear of bubbling cauldrons.

"Have a seat, Trevor!" Miss Plimp said from behind him. Even her perfume was perky—she smelled like a mixture of cotton candy and grape Fun Dip. She must have graduated at the top of her class.

Trevor nodded and carefully sat down in a small, uncomfortable metal chair that seemed better suited for a second grader.

Small metal chairs? But the ones in the waiting area looked so comfy, Trevor thought. Probably just to lure students in here. This may be a trap.

Miss Plimp settled into a wide, plush rocking chair behind her desk. She sighed, then smiled, then sighed again, then added a little head tilt. Then . . . nothing.

Am I supposed to talk first?

Trevor cleared his throat. "Am I supposed to . . . Do you want me to . . . Look, if you don't mind me saying, that poster of Mittens hanging over that cauldron is unnerving."

Miss Plimp looked it over proudly. "It's from the dollar store!"

Trevor wanted to tell her she should have paid a few bucks more for a less disturbing poster, but instead he asked, "So . . . why am I here?"

She folded her arms. "It's been a few weeks since school started, and I wanted to see how things were going."

"You do this with all the seventh graders?" Somehow he knew the answer to this already.

"Well . . . no. Just the extra . . . special ones." She gave him a warm smile.

Trevor looked around the room and noticed that on one wall there weren't any pictures of kittens, just framed diplomas of all her college degrees—which he found reassuring. Since he was in the counselor's office and there were multiple motivating (and yet also terrifying) posters telling him to hang in there, and she had many college degrees, Trevor felt comfortable enough to go ahead and just let it all out. "See, I have this problem," he said.

Miss Plimp tapped at a folder. "I've seen your permanent record."

"Libby is running for class president—"

"Apparently, we have some new rules because of you."

"I had to run against her, but I don't know if I can win—"

"But it says in your record that you worry a lot."

Miss Plimp didn't seem to want to hear about the problem with the election. "But I'm trying to get over that worry problem," Trevor said. "It's no big deal, really. Here's the *real* problem. I've been trying—"

Miss Plimp flipped open the folder. "It says in here you worry about the plant watering schedule and getting peanut butter stuck to the roof of your mouth and slipping on hallway floors after they've been mopped and—"

Trevor hung his head. "Too much peanut butter at once can be a tricky thing."

"But I didn't call you in here to talk about peanut butter, Trevor." Miss Plimp took in a long breath and let it out slowly. "I need to know if you had anything to do with the strange smell in the school."

"No! I promise. I mean, I admit to the deodorant and the soda thing, even though I have no idea how those even happened. But *this*?! No way. If anything, Corey Long is trying to set me up."

"Corey? Now, why would a nice young man like him do such a thing?"

"Because he's ev—"

Miss Plimp leaned forward and called out through the open door. "Corey, hon. Come in here."

Whoa. Is this happening?

Sure enough, it was happening. Corey Long suddenly peeked his head around the corner. "Yes, Miss Plimp?"

Trevor gripped his small chair. "He—who—why—" he said, clearly not making much sense.

"Corey comes by and dusts my cat figurines during his study hall time when he's done with his work," she explained. "He's *so* helpful."

Trevor twisted around so that his back was facing Corey. "But he probably heard everything I just said!"

Miss Plimp nodded. "I hope so. We need to clear the air between you boys." She looked up and waved him over. "Corey, come have a seat."

Trevor sat back and stared at his feet as Corey sauntered in and plopped down in the small, metal seat next to him.

With his heart racing like a rabbit, Trevor did his best not to break out in a sweat. Or hives. Or both. So instead, just like he'd done in the cafeteria, he focused on the exit sign above the door. At least he could possibly make it through this by facing the opposite direction.

"Boys, I want you to turn your chairs and face each other." Miss Plimp looked over at Trevor. "That was a strange sound to make. Are you all right?"

He didn't realize he'd gasped quite so loudly. And strangely. "Sorry."

Reluctantly, they dragged their chairs toward each other, scraping the legs on the tile floor. Miss Plimp squinted until the harsh noise was over and then smiled pleasantly. "Trevor says he didn't cause the smell in the school. But he says you're telling everyone he did. Is that true, Corey?"

"Me?" Corey pressed his hand to his chest—the innocent-as-can-be stance. "Naw, I didn't blame him for that smell. In fact, that hurts my feelings that he would say that."

Miss Plimp put her hand to her heart, looking as if she were hurt. "Oh, my. Maybe you should apologize, Trevor."

"Apologize?!" Trevor chirped, the word coming out quickly and high-pitched, making him sound more like a chipmunk than a seventh grader.

"Look, I have an idea where the smell is coming from," Corey said calmly as he turned his chair away. "It's probably just a dead animal that's caught in the ventilation duct—they just need to locate the opening where a small rodent may have gotten in."

Miss Plimp laced her fingers together. "That's a brilliant thought, Corey. As always. I'll tell you what. Since you boys need to get your friendship back on track, I'm going to put you on a buddy research team to find the source of that smell. You can meet together after school!"

"That's not necessary—" Corey protested.

Trevor couldn't believe Miss Plimp had just used their two names and the word *team* together in a sentence. He felt dizzy.

"Go write it down on my calico cat wall calendar, please," she told Corey.

"Yes, Miss Plimp." As he passed by Trevor, Corey flashed him a narrow-eyed look that said, *I'll get you for this.*

Fantastic, Trevor thought. An afternoon with Corey Long on a buddy research team trying to locate a dead rat. My life is now *refusing* to get better.

"Okay, Trevor," Miss Plimp said. "What other problems did you say you had? Something about being worried you won't win the election?"

Trevor leaned in closer to her and whispered. "But Corey is right over there. He can hear everything."

"Oh, no. He's on the other side of the room. He can't hear."

"I can't hear a thing," Corey piped in.

"See?" Miss Plimp grinned.

Trevor wasn't about to tell her his problems in front of Corey Long, but he had to say something to get out of there.

Glancing at the front of Miss Plimp's desk, Trevor finally came up with exactly the right words to get dismissed. "Miss Plimp, I'm going to adopt a cat."

She nodded. "I do believe you're cured, Trevor Jones. Good luck in the debate today!" Miss Plimp said, feeling very proud of her top-of-the-class counseling skills.

Cindy Applegate

Waiting to head
into the debate,
not worried,
not that much

1:27 p.m.

Okay, so this debate thing? I'm not worried, not that much. Even though I didn't actually practice or anything because I've been so busy on the phone with the customer service department at OvernighT-shirts!com.

They did NOT give us a refund for the T-shirts that were ruined by the sprinklers in the cafeteria because—GET THIS—they said it wasn't covered in the warranty. Apparently, if it had been an ACTUAL fire and an ACTUAL fireman had to hose the school down, then they would have given us refunds, but only if there was TV news coverage and if I'd agreed to mention their Web site twice on camera. I guess I should've read the warranty.

Okay, so that's why I'm totally not prepared for the debate, but what do I really need to prepare for anyway?

I mean, Libby will get nervous and ramble on about something ridiculous, like she did last year. And Trevor, well . . . what is he doing? Why is he even IN this campaign? I know we had to make it an even number or something, but still. Weird. How's my hair?

Libby Gardner

Waiting to head
into the debate,
quite anxious

1:28 p.m.

[pacing on and off camera]

Trevor—how could he do this? Try to BEAT me in the election? It was a dumb move on my part to ask Molly without telling him, but this is politics! I was just trying to win. I didn't MEAN to hurt him.

So now I'm nervous.

[more pacing]

I don't know why, but when I'm nervous I ramble, and sometimes not in a good way—I hope I don't do it today, but it's possible when I get up on the stage I will ramble on and on in front of the entire school about plastic bins or hot glue guns or maybe even— What? Oh, it's time to start?

This is bad.

Trevor Jones

Waiting to head into the debate, jittery (very)

1:29 p.m.

[pacing on and off camera]

What am I doing? Why am I even IN this debate?

I may have made a very bad mistake. Sure, I'll probably lose the election, and there's a good chance I will make a total fool of myself in front of the entire school. All because I tried to help Libby.

[narrows eyes]

Libby. How could she do this? All I ever did was try to help her win the election, and she took me for granted.

Forget it. I have to get a grip. This is going to be my moment. I'm going to win this election, and that will help me gain back all my popularity I lost. All while proving to Libby that she can't take advantage of me.

This will be good. Totally good.

That, or a complete disaster.

CHAPTER SEVENTEEN

"**A**S YOUR STUDENT COUNCIL FACULTY ADVISER, I'D LIKE to welcome you to the Westside Middle School student council debate," Mr. Everett announced. All the students had been ushered into the gym and seated in chairs in rows on the floor. The curtains on the stage had been pulled back to reveal three podiums, ready for each of the nervous candidates to take their positions.

Trevor, Cindy, and Libby sat in the front row, along with the eighth grade candidates, waiting for their turn to debate, which was going to take a while since they had to listen to the treasurer, secretary, and vice presidential candidates have their debates first.

Cindy sat between Trevor and Libby, bouncing her knees, chewing gum, and wiggling excessively, which

Trevor found rather annoying. But these distractions were also helpful in avoiding eye contact with Libby. After all, he was about to beat her at this election and he didn't want to feel guilty about it, not one bit. He worried if he actually *looked* at Libby, she might hypnotize him or turn him to stone or—heaven forbid—make him want to talk to her.

It didn't take long before Cindy's excessive wiggling became far too annoying, so he glanced down at the note-filled index card he'd prepared the night before.

TREVOR'S INDEX CARD

- suggest changing school mascot:
wolverines = cool
ninja wolverines = cooler

- mention getting new P.E.
equipment

-NEVER mention the bad smell
wafting through
the school.

During their research, Marty and Trevor had discovered that 99 percent of the time at a student council debate, the candidates were asked, "How would you make your school a better place?"

A little more research revealed that an overwhelming number of students—73 percent—listed getting new gym equipment as their first pick on how to improve their school. With Marty's help, Trevor had rehearsed his answer and he was prepared.

Cindy and Libby were going *down*.

Once the other debates were over, Mr. Everett rang a gold cymbal with his ballpoint pen. "Time for the seventh grade presidential nominees. Cindy, Trevor, and Libby, please bring your poster with you onto the stage and clip it to your podium."

As the candidates stepped up, they each raced for the podium they wanted. Cindy charged ahead for the one in the middle, while Trevor and Libby both went for the one on the right. They ran right into each other—*crash!* The audience broke out into laughter. Libby and Trevor both scrambled to pick up their posters, which had fallen to the floor. When they each had grabbed their own poster, they glanced up and briefly made eye contact for the first time since yesterday.

Trevor's gut reaction was to apologize. Looking at Libby made him want to call off this silent treatment mode, but he didn't. He couldn't—he had a reputation to rebuild.

Libby's initial reaction was to say sorry, too. But in that moment she was too hurt. She was the one who had dreamed of becoming class president, not Trevor. Why was he doing this to her? Running *against* his best friend?

Neither one would go through with actually saying the entire word, but what *did* come out was the beginning of a sorry: *Ssss*. Which essentially meant the two of them hissed at each other for a moment instead of saying apologies.

Then they stood up, raring back like cobras, and after a truly awkward amount of time, Trevor finally retreated and took the podium on the left.

He couldn't believe it—the debate hadn't even started and they'd already hissed at each other like reptiles on the Animal Channel. This was going to be a rough debate. But then Trevor felt a sense of relief when he leaned over and caught a glimpse of the poster Libby had attached to her podium.

Wow, winning this is going to be easier than I thought.

Mr. Everett announced, "There will be two debate questions that you will each answer. Pretty standard stuff."

Trevor stuck his hands in his pockets and took a deep

breath. Looking out at the entire school (some of them clamping their noses because the smell was still quite bad), Trevor was surprised that he wasn't experiencing a panic attack. Standing in front of large crowds had almost always resulted in shortness of breath, chest pain, and the sense that he was going to faint, vomit, and/or die. But not this time. He was going to use this debate to regain all the popularity he'd lost. And he was going to prove to Libby that he was cool enough to run a winning campaign. He was done with being humiliated.

"The first question is this." Mr. Everett paused for dramatic effect, then spoke loudly for even *more* dramatic effect. "Who do you think caused that horrible smell and, as president, how do you plan to help the hazmat crew locate it?"

Public humiliation, welcome back.

Whatever happened to "How will you make your school a better place?" Trevor couldn't believe *this* was the first debate question.

"Cindy, you'll go first."

"Sure, Mr. Everett," Cindy said with a beaming smile. She was looking quite tall since she had managed to bring a step stool onstage with her. She carried the step stool with her for all public speaking—added height was important to her. "I do not believe in spreading rumors, only *facts*. The only way we can find out who is responsible for that smell and not just rudely throw names around is to use the scientific method to determine if Trevor is the cause. And also? As president, I feel we should help the hazmat crew by offering them encouragement and some sandwiches. Thank you!" She grinned and took a bow, wobbling on her step stool.

Mr. Everett scratched his head. "O-kay. Libby, you're next."

Libby wasn't sure how to answer. She had no idea how to find the smell or help a hazmat crew. Her specialty was along the lines of event planning and color coding to make finding things easier. Her other specialty was rambling when she didn't know the answer to something. "I don't know what caused the smell but it could be a chemical or something is broken or old or rotten or *maybe* there is a thief who has planted a smell bomb or there's a refrigerator that has not been cleaned out or . . . or *maybe* it's a combination of all of these things and a thief put a rotten chemical smell bomb in the refrigerator in the teacher's lounge, and so . . . yeah, that's all, thank you."

Mr. Everett paused for a moment to let Libby catch her breath. Once she had returned to a normal, safe breathing pattern, he turned to Trevor. "I guess it's your turn, Mr. Jones."

Trevor's stomach dropped. All eyes were on him as they waited for his response, but they weren't friendly, encouraging looks. No, they were *glares*. Not only did most of the student body believe that Trevor had caused the odor, but now there were a number of rumors circulating as to *how* Trevor had created it. One rumor floating around involved him stashing a rotten Easter egg in the ventilation system, which technically didn't make sense because it was September, but the rumor still persisted. Another involved him and a case of blue cheese dressing, but not many people were buying that one.

Still, Trevor had to find a way to convince them that he had nothing to do with the smell—that they shouldn't assume someone's guilty just because they have a reputation for making mistakes.

But then he realized that that was what he *should* say. He cleared his throat and took a long breath. "Look, I've made mistakes. I spilled soda on the cafeteria floor. And I accidentally sprayed deodorant in Coach Fleming's face. That is all true. And I'm sorry about the new rules and stuff. But just because I made a couple of mistakes doesn't mean I'm bound to keep making them the rest of my life. I didn't cause this smell. That's the truth. The hazmat crew deserves our help and our suggestions if anyone has any. I can start a box. They'd probably like sandwiches, too, but don't put them in the box. Thank you."

Trevor stepped back and looked down at his feet. And then he heard the sound. Clapping. They were clapping for *him*. The students weren't loud—it wasn't an ovation, but it was respectable. And Trevor felt like he'd made the right decision in running for president.

He was ready for the second question. His research showed that in 85 percent of student council debates, presidential candidates were asked this question: What is your campaign platform?

Mr. Everett cleared his throat and spoke loudly into his microphone. "And the next question is . . ."

Dramatic pause.

"Where would you go on vacation if you had all the money in the world?"

Oh, come on. Trevor understood that Mr. Everett wanted them to establish their character and all, but weren't they just supposed to answer questions about their platform and school changes? The standard debate questions! Shouldn't they talk about P.E. equipment? Discuss lunch food items? Wouldn't that make more sense?

Trevor swallowed hard. Hopefully he wouldn't have to go first.

"Trevor, you're first."

Awesome.

He figured he should say something cool and also something sort of responsible to show he'd make a good president. So he first considered the Bahamas, but that sounded like he would be a president who would frivolously spend money. Then he thought maybe he should go on vacation to visit his family, because that would be fun *and* respectable.

He quickly glanced out to the audience and saw Marty in the back row mouthing some words to him. But he was too far away and Trevor couldn't quite make out what he was trying to say. With time running out, he quickly went through his list of cousins, but only his cousin Charlie with the tractor stuck in his mind.

"Topeka."

The audience laughed, and it took a moment for Mr. Everett to get them settled down. Trevor couldn't believe *that* was the first town that came to mind for his dream vacation. After all, he had relatives in New York City! Not actually *in* the city, just outside. But still!

"Topeka . . . My cousin has a John Deere tractor . . .

They raise elk . . . grow bean sprouts," he started to explain, but the audience laughed even more.

He looked over and saw Libby with her hand covering her mouth. Was she holding back a snicker?! And Cindy was laughing but not covering up her mouth at all, letting all of Westside and the whole world see her amusement in the situation.

It hit him that this debate was starting to slip away from him, along with some shreds of his dignity.

FOUND IN TREVOR'S NOTEBOOK

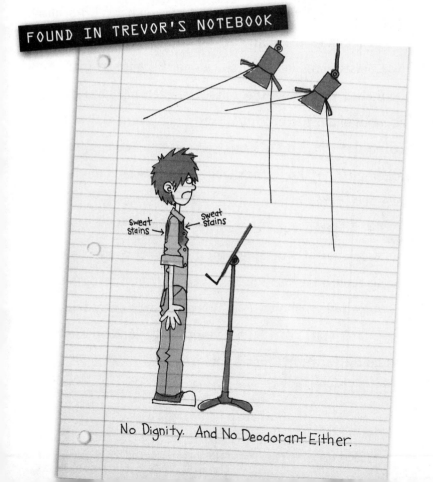

sweat stains →

← sweat stains

No Dignity. And No Deodorant Either.

Mr. Everett then moved on to Libby.

She fanned herself with her hand so she could take a moment to focus. She needed to think of something cool, like maybe zip-lining in Costa Rica or snowboarding in Aspen. But she didn't know anything about those things because she had never done any of those things.

Since her mom worked a lot, most of her school vacations were spent at home. So she talked about the first thing that came to mind—the thing she *did* know something about. "I'd spend my vacation where I normally do—at home reorganizing my bedroom. I like to make sure I use plastic bins that are stackable. Because, if you think about it, if the bins AREN'T stackable, aren't you just making more of a disaster for yourself? Am I right?" She figured adding the *Am I right* would give it that cool touch. She looked out, hoping to see some smiling faces, but the audience just stared at her.

She fidgeted with the corner of her poster. "Um. You can even store them under your bed. For a good storage-saving technique. And so . . . yeah. Okay, thank you." As her voice faded, she wished she could fade away with it.

"Thank you, Libby," Mr. Everett said. "And where would you go on vacation, Miss Applegate?"

Cindy pushed up on her tiptoes. "My choice for a

vacation spot? There's Hawaii, which rocks in the snorkeling and luau departments, but the beach sand really isn't as white as I'd like it. Can't they bleach it or something? Okay and also? There's Disney World . . . You can't go wrong with Space Mountain. But if you have to go with your little brother and all his creepy friends, then it's a full-on nightmare on a stick, so I'd have to go with one of those cruises where they have babysitters on board for your little brother. Oh, and vote for me, Westside!"

"And that concludes our seventh grade presidential debate. Very eye-opening information," Mr. Everett said to the audience. "Next up will be the eighth grade debate. Please place your votes in the box on your way out, and we'll announce the winners during the last class of the day."

Libby, Trevor, and Cindy grabbed their posters and headed offstage to go to class. They didn't make eye contact, didn't say a word, just gathered their things and calmly walked away from each other.

Trevor worried he'd answered that vacation question strangely.

Libby wished she hadn't talked about organizing bins so much.

And Cindy just smiled, because she knew she'd nailed it.

Nancy Polanski

7th grader
As she exits
the gym

2:10 p.m.

Who did I vote for for class president? It's a secret ballot so I'm technically not allowed to disclose the name of that person, but I WILL say that one person in particular did do a great job, in my opinion. He was funny and to the point and handsome and I liked ALL of his answers.

But no, I can't tell you who I voted for. You'll just have to wait for the results like the rest of us.

Jamie Jennison

7th grader
As she exits
the gym

2:11 p.m.

Me? Oh, I voted for Libby! Though I was disappointed in her discussion of room cleaning, I was VERY impressed with her honesty about not knowing where the smell is coming from. I like the truth.

Plus, she really is the most organized candidate. Have you ever seen the inside of her locker? Even our school librarian is impressed. In fact, I think that should be part of the debate—a locker competition. Kind of like the swimsuit competition in Miss America? But with lockers!

I mean, you could really learn a lot about a person by judging what's inside their locker. Rumor has it Cindy's locker has a live kitten in there. I don't believe that, but there is some faux fur sticking out of it. And I'm not sure I want to know what's inside Trevor's locker—he always seems like he's in a rush.

Some doors are probably better left closed. Am I right?

Baker Twins

7th graders
As they exit
the gym

2:12 p.m.

Brian: I voted for Cindy.

Brad: I voted for Cindy.

[turn and look at each other, confused]

Brian: You too?

Brad: Wait, we AGREED on something? Why'd you vote for her?

Brian: She told me she'd give me a pack of Hubba Bubba Sour Apple.

Brad: That's weird. She came up to me and told me she'd up it to TWO packs of Hubba Bubba Sour Apple if I convinced some other people to vote for her, too.

Brian: Huh.

Brad: Huh.

Brian: Aww, dude, she probably thinks we're the same person.

Brad: This is embarrassing.

Molly Decker

As she exits
the gym

2:13 p.m.

Me? I didn't vote for anyone. How could I? Trevor and Libby haven't talked to me since THE BIG BLOWUP. And I'm not exactly excited about Cindy's idea to bleach all the sand in Hawaii, so . . . no, I left my ballot empty.

I'm not sure what I can do to get them talking to me again, or if they ever will. I guess I shouldn't have gotten involved—that's what I've always done before, just collected "things," and life was just fine. No weirdness.

Sometimes I wish my dad would just let me go back to collecting things. But he says I have to make friends and "keep" them.

[scuffs boot on the floor]

He didn't tell me how.

CHAPTER EIGHTEEN

LANGUAGE ARTS WAS TREVOR'S LAST CLASS OF THE DAY, which was when the election results would be announced. It was also a class he shared with both Libby and Cindy. The three of them had very purposely avoided all forms of contact—eye, verbal, of the note-passing variety—for the first thirty minutes. It had been awkward.

But Trevor was tired of all the awkwardness.

This is ridiculous. I should talk to Libby—tell her what I'm thinking. There's no reason why we can't be civil at least.

He stood to approach Libby's desk, but that's when he noticed her organizing and reorganizing the books in her backpack. Not good. This behavior was a sure sign that she was upset—*very* upset.

Once, after he beat her at level nineteen of Star Invaders, she organized and reorganized all the *National Geographic* magazines (from 1979 to present) on the bookshelf at his house. That had actually worked out pretty well for him, because later, when he'd had a homework assignment, he was able to find an article on polar bear habitats within minutes. So sometimes her "upset behavior" was helpful.

But probably not in this case.

The intercom crackled and Vice Principal Decker said, "Students, the votes are in and I have the results of the student council election. Seventh graders, your new treasurer is Noah Dawson. Secretary is Jessie Weston. Vice president is Alecia Sanchez. And your president is . . ."

There was a shuffling of papers.

"It appears we have . . . Wow. We apparently have . . . a three-way tie."

Both Libby and Trevor snapped their heads up and looked at each other. Neither said anything or eyebrowed anything, just looked blankly. Because they simply didn't know what to say. A *tie*?

"I will now consult the handbook to see how to handle this," Vice Principal Decker explained. They could hear him flipping through papers.

Libby crossed her hands in her lap and looked down.

She no longer wanted to make eye contact with Trevor, since she knew a tie meant this election wasn't over yet.

"Ah, here we go," Vice Principal Decker announced. "Section two of article seven point four says that if there is a tie, *another* debate and election shall be held, preferably the next day and preferably right before the weekend, to minimize the crying at school. Since tomorrow is a Friday, that settles it. We will have one final debate and vote at two thirty p.m. Now our eighth grade results . . ."

Trevor didn't bother listening. He couldn't believe it. Debate *again*? All he knew was that spending the previous night researching what questions to expect had gotten him nowhere. And now he was going to have to answer Mr. Everett's bizarre questions all over again? At that moment all he could think about was getting out of that class and going home—he needed to figure out what to do.

"I'm here for Trevor Jones." Suddenly, Miss Plimp had appeared at the door. And slouching next to her was Corey Long. His face was flushed and he looked as though he'd been dragged there by his ear.

Mr. Lewis, Trevor's language arts teacher, looked up and called out across the room. "What do you need him for?"

Everyone turned and looked.

"Corey and Trevor are going to be Research Buddies today!" Miss Plimp said with her usual excitement. "The two of them are going to locate the source of that smell!"

Trevor had forgotten that today was the day he'd get to spend a glorious afternoon rat hunting side-by-side with Corey Long.

Maybe it wouldn't take too long.

Trevor didn't know why Miss Plimp was pulling him out of class early rather than letting them do this after school. Why the rush? But then again, the sooner he got out of there, the sooner this humiliating moment could get started. And then hopefully be over with.

The students in the class snickered as Trevor gathered his things and left the room. Miss Plimp led the boys away from the class and said, "I wanted you boys to get an early start ahead of the crowds. This way you can chitchat and it won't be so noisy! Now, you two go hunting around and find that awful smell. But most important, have fun!"

She clapped three times, her signature move before something big was about to start. She trotted back down the hallway as if she was quite pleased with herself for finding a way to get Trevor and Corey to be friends.

But once Miss Plimp was out of earshot, Corey leaned over and said, "I'm not doing any 'buddy research.' Forget it. You go your way, I'll go mine. I have a plan anyway."

"A plan?"

"Yeah. I already have it all set up with those hazmat goons. If someone gives a suggestion, they get to throw a ball at the hazmat dunk tank. Like at a carnival or something. Everyone will love it—I will go down in history as the most awesome eighth grader ever in Westside history."

Trevor cringed at his use of the word *history* twice in his sentence. But then it hit him that he'd found a flaw in Corey's "most awesome idea ever." "But how are you going to get your hands on one of those dunk tanks?" Trevor was pleased with himself for pointing this problem out. Corey clearly hadn't thought through his plans.

"My dad has a dunk tank they use for fund-raisers down at the Lions' Lodge. He already said I could borrow it." Corey poked Trevor on the shoulder, rather hard. "It's better than some stupid tip box."

So Corey *did* think through his plans. Good to know, thought Trevor.

But before Trevor could agree with him and tell him a dunk tank actually sounded awesome, he heard the sound of squeaky thick soles heading toward them—it was one of the hazmat crew members.

"Dwayne!" Corey exclaimed.

"Corey! What's up, kid?" Dwayne's voice echoed through his mask as he high-fived Corey.

"I've got lots of plans for that dunk tank I was telling you about," Corey explained as the two of them walked off down the hall together, leaving Trevor alone.

Trevor's jaw tightened—Corey was the guy with the stellar reputation, and this dunk tank idea was only going to make it better. Why did guys like him always seem to win in the end? Corey was a professional jerk and everyone respected him—it didn't seem fair.

Trevor stormed over to his locker, yanked the door open, and threw his English book in as hard as he could. No one else was around, and it felt good to throw something that hard, actually.

But he heard a strange *thud* when he threw the book. Peering in, he pulled back papers and books (it was quite a jumbled mess in there), and he noticed there was a hole in the back corner.

He pushed on the wall of his locker and part of it gave way. Apparently, his old, rusted-out locker was connected to a duct, like part of a ventilation system. And when he took in a deep breath, he was overtaken by a stench. His stomach lurched from the horrible mixture of old tires and rotten fish and moldy bread.

He grabbed his nose as he leaned over slightly to let in a glimmer of light from the hallway so he could figure out what was causing the smell.

Instantly, he recognized what it was.

Trevor Jones

Standing far away
from his locker,
talking with his
nose clamped

2:55 p.m.

My tuna sandwich. THAT'S what was causing the smell. *MY* tuna sandwich—the one I didn't eat on Monday so I could look cool at Jake Jacobs's lunch table. It got caught between my locker and the wall, and that's how the smell got into the ventilation system, and that's why the entire school is now crawling with guys in hazmat suits.

Because of ME.

[bends over]

Breathe, Trevor. Breathe.

And I went up onstage in front of the ENTIRE student body and told them I didn't have anything to do with this.

If it weren't for the fact that this ridiculous story is MY story, then yeah . . . it'd be pretty funny.

But right now, I don't see how this could get any worse.

CHAPTER NINETEEN

NORMALLY, TREVOR WOULD ENJOY HIS AFTERNOON ride home on the bus. The wind blowing through the windows. The laughter. The bouncy seat in the back. Even with Libby not speaking to him he might have found a way to have a decent enough ride home.

But now the biggest stench disaster in Westside history could only be blamed on him, and he had no idea what to do about it. When the final dismissal bell had rung, he'd left the sandwich in his locker, since he didn't want to get caught with it. At that point it's possible that panic set in. He'd slammed his locker door shut and hurried down the hall, glancing nervously at his classmates and wondering exactly how he was going to handle this new problem. Help. He needed help. And if there was anyone who could solve a dilemma like this, it was Libby.

But Libby wasn't ready to talk to Trevor—this whole debate do-over was just too devastating. She'd hardly gotten up the confidence to get through the first debate, so how could she possibly handle another one? She couldn't. She'd made a total fool of herself during the first debate. What was she thinking? Her dream vacation was to *reorganize her bedroom*? And while she didn't feel that Cindy's answers had had any substance, at least she hadn't rambled on and on about stackable containers. And Trevor . . . Trevor! Even he had done better than she had. Sure, his Topeka response had been a little tragic, but his answer to the first question was honest.

Still, Libby couldn't believe that Trevor was actually trying to take class president away from her. What kind of best friend would do that? Libby really didn't want to talk to him about it—not now and maybe not ever.

When Trevor got on the bus he spotted Libby sitting near the front. Even though she was looking straight ahead, ignoring him, he hoped they could take a break from fighting for a minute.

He sat down a few seats behind her. "Lib!" he called out. But she just shook her head, kept facing forward, and refused to look back.

Clearly, a quality bus talk wasn't going to happen. He was going to have to convince her to talk to him on the walk home. When the bus pulled to their stop, Trevor hurried off to catch up with her. "Lib, I need your help. Seriously. Can we just forget about this election thing for a minute? Please!"

But again, she didn't talk to him, didn't look his way, didn't glance back at him, and didn't even toss him a wave good-bye when he got to the bottom of his driveway—something she'd always done forever since the beginning of time.

FOUND IN TREVOR'S NOTEBOOK

See? Ever since we were dinosaurs.

Trevor realized that not only was he going to have to deal with the biggest public relations disaster in middle school history *all by himself*, but also that something far worse had just happened right there at the end of his driveway.

He had just lost his best friend.

He kicked a rock and headed into his house, where he hoped his mother would be waiting for him. If anyone could tell him what to do, it was his mother. He wasn't sure if that was a good thing or not, but he was about to find out.

"Mom, I need your help," he said as he bolted through the front door.

Ms. Jones was in the living room doing her *Tae Kwon Do Navy SEALs Aerobics Dance* video. She adjusted her sparkly pink headband. "Trevor, can you talk while I do my prayer pose predator squats?" She bent one knee, but not *too* far, being careful not to overstretch her newly purchased camouflage yoga pants—good for concealment *and* light exercise.

Trevor settled on the couch while his mother continued her workout. "So I sort of . . . *did* something today."

"Good test score?" she asked, a little out of breath.

"Not exactly." Trevor winced and prepared for impact. "I ran for seventh grade class president."

Ms. Jones stopped mid–predator squat. "Trevor, that's wonderful!" Then she stood up and tilted her head, sweat dripping from her temple. "Oh, wait . . ."

Prepare for impact.

"Isn't that Libby's—"

"Lifelong dream. Yeah, pretty much." He held a hand up. "Mom, I can explain—"

Ms. Jones dried herself off with a towel and sat down next to Trevor. She could sense that his running for student class president was not something he was particularly happy about.

Trevor started at the beginning and told his mom everything. "And now Libby won't talk to me, which means I've lost my best friend, AND it turns out I'm the cause of the bad smell at school—it was my tuna sandwich. And I have no idea how to fix all this."

Ms. Jones tilted her head. "The smell . . . You mean that was *you?*"

"How do you know about the smell?"

"It's been all over the Internet. E-mails from the school, e-vites for a town meeting, and now this post on the PTA home page. Such a fabulous idea. Don't you think?" She turned to her computer.

Trevor plopped his head in his hands. Corey Long was

Westside PTA!
Your kid's got at least half a chance!

Help us find the source of the stench at Westside Middle School!

Give a suggestion, get 3 FREE balls for the Hazmat Dunk Tank!

(Fabulous idea courtesy of Corey Long)

now charming the entire Parent Teacher Association. Next, the world.

Through his fingers, he mumbled, "What do you think I should do, Mom?" He looked up at her, noticing she'd taken off her sparkly headband, and her forehead was red and splotchy, like she'd been thinking really hard.

"Do you think I should tell everyone I caused the smell?"

She shrugged. "This is a tricky one. You have to balance your reputation with knowing when to tell the truth."

"Exactly." He leaned forward, excited that he was about to get the help he needed with this dilemma.

She squeezed his shoulder. "Fortunately, I raised you right. You'll know what to do when the time comes."

Trevor sighed. Not the answer he was hoping for. What was the point in spilling his guts to her if she didn't *tell* him what to do and *when* to do it?

Ms. Jones ruffled his hair. "Aw, Trevor. I usually only give you these when you've done something good." She hopped up and jogged into the kitchen, then reached into the drawer and tossed him a Raspberry Zinger from across the room. "But sometimes these are helpful when you're feeling down, too."

"Thanks, Mom." He ripped open the package. But after a couple of bites, he realized it would take a mountain of Zingers to solve this problem.

That evening, six doors down, Mrs. Gardner was serving her famous baked chicken. "How'd the election go today, Libby?"

Libby didn't say a word. She just picked at her chicken with her fork, not taking a bite.

"What's wrong? Is it the oregano? I knew I should have backed off a little—"

"No, Mom. I adore your chicken. It's just . . ." She dropped her fork and rested her chin in the palm of her hand. "I can't believe Trevor is deliberately trying to hurt my feelings."

Mrs. Gardner tightened the top on the oregano and sat down next to her. "Hurt your feelings? I don't understand. He was here just the other night helping you get ready for the debate."

"But then he found out I asked Molly to be my campaign manager, and he got all mad and decided to try and *win* student class president. Which ended up in a three-way tie, and now we have to do another debate. But I don't have any good slogans or posters or passion. . . ." She dropped her head. "I don't know what's wrong with me, Mom. I used to be so good at these things, and now I'm worried I'll never think of the right words. I wish I could win because of my ideas."

Mrs. Gardner patted her on the back. She felt bad that Libby was feeling this way, but she needed to get some facts straight first. "Honey? You . . . you *replaced* Trevor?"

Libby looked up, her face flushed. Not *replaced* . . . just more like *added*. But her mother kept staring at her with a blank face. This was not making sense. "See, here's the thing. Cousin Luke told me my campaign had to be cool, and he laughed at my posters, which was why I threw them away, so I needed to find a manager who could help me come up with a cool campaign, cool slogan, cool everything."

Mrs. Gardner laughed. Laughed a lot.

"Mom, what's so funny?"

"Your cousin Luke? Honey, he's in a band. He thinks *everything* has to be cool. He thinks toothpaste has to be cool."

"But he won his seventh *and* eighth grade class president elections by coming up with cool campaigns," Libby replied.

"Is that what he told you? He won because no one else would run for office—the principal appointed him."

Libby smiled a little. "You mean—"

Mrs. Gardner patted Libby's hand. "Don't listen to Luke—I think he may have eaten a little too much dirt when he was a kid. Rely on your own instincts. And your friends—the ones who are there in the moments that matter. You already have one of those friends . . . but you seem to have forgotten that." She pushed her chair back and stood up. "Stay here. I want to show you something."

Libby fiddled with the hem of her shirt while she waited for her mom, whom she could hear rummaging through something down the hall. What was she doing?

Moments later, her mom reappeared, posters in one hand and a trash can in the other. "The other night, when Trevor was here to help you clean your room, he did some things I haven't told you about."

Libby sat back in her chair. What was going on? She felt a flutter in her stomach.

"Those posters that you threw away?" Mrs. Gardner smiled sweetly. "He pulled them out and asked me to save them for you. He thought they were good—*really* good."

Libby grabbed one of the posters and unrolled it. There were a few stains, but it wasn't completely ruined. She could still use it, and after looking it over, she realized Trevor was right—the poster actually was pretty good.

"But he *did* throw away this." Mrs. Gardner held out the trash can for Libby to see inside. "It's a note from Jessica Lymon." Her mom reached out and tucked Libby's hair behind her ear. "Trevor told me you don't need it anymore. And he thinks maybe the problem is you're throwing away the wrong things."

Libby felt a rush of warmth, and her face filled with a huge smile. She suddenly felt maybe she could win this election because of her ideas. Trevor had known that all along—if only she had listened to him. She couldn't believe she had told him he wasn't cool enough to run her campaign for her. What kind of best friend would do that? Not a good one.

Libby tucked her poster under her arm and kissed her mom on the forehead. "I have a big, fat apology to make, Mom. Let's hope it's not too late."

WESTSIDE
MIDDLE SCHOOL
DO-OVER
DEBATE DAY

CHAPTER TWENTY

WHILE WAITING FOR THE BUS, TREVOR WAS EXPECTING more silence from Libby. And he was also expecting a not-so-stellar day ahead. Maybe one of his worst. He'd thought about his mom's advice on how to handle the smell situation—that he'd know what to do when the time came. Apparently, he needed *more* time, because he had no idea what to do. And really he didn't understand how time would fix this anyway.

In the distance, he saw Libby practically skipping up the street toward him. At least it *looked* like she was headed toward him. He glanced around, quickly measuring angles to see if she was walking happily toward someone else. But sure enough, Trevor's initial guess was right, as she strutted right up to him.

"I have something important to tell you." She gently grabbed him by the arm and pulled him away from the line of kids.

Trevor was confused. She was actually using words with him? "Why are you talking to me now?"

She pulled out the poster tucked under her arm. "My mom told me you saved it from the trash."

He was glad she brought out the poster he had saved for her, but mostly he wanted to hide that his face was now turning spaghetti-sauce red, so he looked down at his feet. It didn't occur to him that she would be all nice and make some big scene about it at the bus stop.

Libby bent down to catch his eye. "And my mom *also* told me that you threw away that note Jessica Lymon wrote me. I can't believe you did that!"

He jerked his head up, not even worried that she was seeing the dark red color of his face. Was she mad? The last thing he'd wanted to do was upset her by throwing away that note—he just didn't want her to be reminded of something that made her feel bad. "Lib, don't be mad. I didn't mean to—"

She put a hand on his shoulder and smiled. "Trevor Jones. It was the nicest thing a friend has ever done for me. I don't even know why I held on to it for so long.

But seeing it crumpled up in the bottom of the trash, and knowing that you threw it away because you really believe in me . . . I don't know, I think it was the push I needed. I should trust my own instincts."

Trevor grinned. "Jessica Lymon didn't know what she was talking about. The girl is missing a solar panel or two, if you ask me."

Libby giggled and said, "I'm sorry—for everything. I never should have asked Molly to be my manager. I didn't need someone who was cool, just someone who was there for me. And that's you—it's always you. So I'm an idiot for asking you to staple things for me. And next year, I'm giving you the title of chief officer. Or lieutenant." She smirked. "Commander?"

"Master Trevor will do, thank you very much."

She stuck her hand out. "Good luck today in the debate. If you win, no hard feelings. I promise."

But so far, this was *her* lifelong dream, not his. He couldn't take it away from her. "What do you mean, if I win? I'm not going to win."

"Sure, you did great yesterday. You have a really good chance—"

"Listen up, Libby Gardner. I'm going to throw the debate. I don't actually want to be class president; I was just angry with you. There is no way I'm going to go up on that stage today and try to win. You've been preparing for this your whole life, and you *deserve* to win."

Libby twirled her hair in her fingers, looking worried. "But if you go up there and lose on purpose, it might hurt your reputation. I don't want people to think you're not cool, Trevor—because you are."

"I'm going to do it because it's not cool, and I don't care. That's the definition of cool. Molly told me that, actually."

Libby raised a brow. "Okay, then. It's not the kind of help I was looking for from Molly, but I'm glad she's being helpful somehow." She crossed her arms and sighed, a real sigh—not a fake one.

"What's wrong?" Trevor asked.

"I'm just really worried that Mr. Everett is going to ask again about that ridiculous smell and how to find it. How am I supposed to know? At least you came up with that good idea for the smell tip box."

The smell!

Trevor's mom said he would know what to do when the time was right, and he realized that the time had just come.

The two ideas—the smell and Libby winning the election—crashed together in his brain like two awesome ingredients in a candy bar, and instantaneously he created a plan. A really good one, too, he thought.

"I have a plan, Lib. Remember yesterday when I tried to talk to you on our way home from school?"

"When I ignored you. Gosh, I'm sorry—"

He waved her off. "It's okay. Look, what I was trying to tell you is that I know where the smell is coming from."

She laced her fingers together. "You do?! That's great!"

"Not *all* great." He stepped back a little before he unloaded the truth. "Because *I'm* the one who caused the smell."

Libby dropped her hands. "But you told everyone—"

"That was before I knew it was me. Yesterday, I opened my locker and found a hole in the back. And the tuna sandwich my mom packed for me on Monday . . . was rotting in it."

Libby squinted. "Eww. That's disgusting."

"Totally. But I have a plan. That disgusting sandwich is going to win you this election."

Trevor Jones

At the bus stop
Out of earshot
of Libby

7:55 a.m.

I told her to get up on that stage and blame the smell on me. If SHE is the one who finds the source of the smell, then she'll be a hero, and they'll have to vote for her. I really don't think they can take the stench any longer.

So yeah, my reputation is going to be pulverized. But you know what? I don't really care anymore. Because what matters is that Libby's dream comes true. That's the whole reason I got into politics, right?

And I guess I have to admit that Luke does know what he's talking about. Popularity *is* fleeting—at least for me.

But like Wilson said, I was lucky mine lasted for almost a week. So I should be happy, I guess.

I'm sure my happiness will kick in anytime now.

Libby Gardner

At the bus stop
Out of earshot
of Trevor

7:56 a.m.

I can't believe he'd do this for me. Put his reputation on the line just so I can win the election?
It's the nicest thing ever. TOO nice, in fact.

And that's why I'm not going to do it.

I have a plan of my own. I think I can fix this
so that no one gets their reputation ruined.

[cringes a little]

At least I hope not.

CHAPTER TWENTY-ONE

TREVOR ENTERED **W**ESTSIDE KNOWING THAT AT EXACTLY two thirty p.m. that day, he would join the middle school Hall of Fame for the quickest rise and fall in popularity of a seventh grader. The entire school would learn that he was the cause of the horrible stench. And it was highly likely that Vice Principal Decker would then create yet another new school rule because of Trevor. Something like: No more fun. Or breathing.

Letting Libby do this was all his idea. And his popularity—maybe even all of his future popularity from now on—would be completely obliterated. Trevor wondered if he had totally lost his mind.

As he made his way to homeroom, he prayed for a freak sandstorm or a UFO sighting or a Sasquatch appearance to distract everyone from what was going to happen later that day.

But when he saw Libby happily strolling down the hall toward homeroom, looking as if she had it all figured out, he was relieved that she had finally turned it around. If anyone was meant to be class president, it was Libby. So if admitting he was to blame for the smell in a humiliating public manner was what it would take to help her win, then it was the right choice.

Time to move forward with the plan.

Trevor made it through his morning classes without much incident, but when it came time for lunch, he was reminded of the horror that was to come.

Through the cafeteria windows he saw Corey organizing a group of kids on the blacktop. They were happily dropping suggestions in a box, then throwing balls at a target. The hazmat dunk tank.

Munching on chicken nuggets, Trevor stood at the window watching everyone high-five Corey as they happily dunked the hazmat crew.

"This is bad news." Marty had walked up. "Corey's dunk tank is overshadowing your suggestion box idea. We need to come up with something better. Like straight A's for whoever finds the smell. Or maybe—"

"I've decided to lose, actually."

Marty scratched his head. "Why would you want to do that?"

"Libby. I can't take this away from her—she's my best friend."

Marty squinted at him. "You mean you're going to get up on that stage and lose the debate on purpose—making a complete fool of yourself in the process—just so that Libby can win?"

Trevor shrugged as he took a bite of chicken nugget. "Yep."

Marty shoved his hands in his pockets and thought this over as he stared out the windows at the hazmat crew being dunked. He couldn't believe Trevor would do all this just to help Libby win. But he had to admit it was a pretty epic thing to do. "All right, Trevor." He clamped down on his shoulder. "Then I hope you lose the debate horribly . . . the worst smackdown ever."

Trevor grinned. "Thanks, Marty. Thanks a lot."

Marty walked on to sit with his eighth grade friends. Trevor headed toward Libby's normal table so he could sit with her. But to his surprise, Libby wasn't there. Odd. He tapped Jamie Jennison on the shoulder. "Jamie, do you know where Libby is?"

"I haven't seen her. She didn't show up for lunch."

He wondered what she was up to.

Knowing there had to be a way to get the smell issue resolved for Trevor, Libby put her plan into action and went in search of help. And she knew exactly the person who could help her: Wilson. Trevor always seemed to get solid advice from him, so maybe Wilson would be willing to help her if it was for a good reason.

Libby rounded the corner toward the office, and that's when she saw him. Along a wall in the lobby near the front office, Wilson was setting up a folding table and chairs.

She waved. "Wilson! I'm Libby—Trevor's friend."

Wilson glanced up—no smile, seeming very serious—and looked her over. "The organized one. Trevor's talked of you."

"What are you setting up this table for?" she asked.

"Confession. See, those hazmat goons can't locate the source of the smell, and they think asking the students for suggestions and setting up a dunk tank like some carnival game will work. But *I'll* be the one to find out where that smell is coming from." He glanced around and lowered his voice. "Then we'll prove to Decker who the *real* expert is around here." He sat down and folded his arms, then leaned

across the table. "I've been studying the students' behavior, thinking it would be obvious who caused the smell. But for some reason, none of them have given themselves away yet. So now I'm sure it's this bulb. THAT'S how I'll find the smell. It'll lure in a student, and once they're under the glow of this interrogation bulb . . . it's inevitable—they'll fess up."

This was perfect, Libby thought. Wilson wanted to discover the source of the smell so he could prove himself to Vice Principal Decker. And Libby could lead him right to it.

She pulled up a chair and sat down under the bright light of his interrogation bulb. "Wilson, I have to tell you something."

"This seat is for students who want to admit they know the truth about the smell. If you want to talk about organizing supplies, we can talk after school."

Libby leaned in and whispered, "But I *do* know the truth. You want to show Decker and those hazmat guys that the *real* expert around here is the man in charge of custodial support, right?"

Wilson lifted a brow. "I'm listening."

"Then follow me. I have a locker to show you."

Wilson

Standing near
Trevor's locker,
looking pleased
with himself

1:05 p.m.

Ah, yes. The tuna-sandwich-stuck-in-a-locker problem. Saw it back in '98—except that one had extra mayo. We had to evacuate the building.

[shakes head]

Libby and I hatched a win-win plan for all of us. She'll call me up onstage during the debate and I'll tell everyone I've discovered where the smell is coming from.

[holds up a sack]

See, I wrapped Trevor's sandwich up in this burlap sack, and I'm going to tell them I found a rabid long-tailed bush rat—a real SICK one—from Madagascar that was emitting the horrible stench.

I'll probably even wiggle the sack around for added effect.

So I'm willing to do Libby this favor—Decker will see that I CAN handle these matters. Plus,

there's no way I could make Trevor suffer anymore—
that kid's already lost enough of his dignity this
week.

[lifts a brow]

My guess is this will make for our most interesting do-over debate ever.

CHAPTER TWENTY-TWO

IT WAS TIME FOR THE SECOND PRESIDENTIAL DEBATE, BUT today was completely different. This time, Trevor was going to help his friend win by throwing the debate. And Libby was confident and ready to take on Mr. Everett's questions.

Cindy, though, felt just the same as she did yesterday, and wondered why this was all taking so long.

"Students, take your seats!" Mr. Everett called out over the microphone as he rubbed his temple. He'd been in charge of running student council debates for the past five years, but this do-over debate was proving exceptionally challenging. He could feel a migraine coming.

"Trevor, Cindy, and Libby, please take the stage for our first question," he announced.

And just like yesterday, the three of them took their places on the stage behind their podiums. Except today, Libby and Trevor didn't bump into each other awkwardly and hiss. Today, Trevor went left and Libby went right, as if they had been choreographed.

The three candidates then went about attaching their posters to the front of their podiums. Libby unrolled one that Trevor had saved from the trash; it was slightly crinkled and stained but completely useable. For the first time in this whole election process, she was feeling hopeful.

LIBBY'S NEW POSTER

GET WITH LiBBY AND GET INVOLVED!

WESTSIDE IS #1!

WESTSIDE IS #1!

But Trevor's hands suddenly went clammy—he was just moments away from the possibility of being asked the question about the smell.

"The first question." Mr. Everett cleared his throat. "The hazmat dunk tank has been very popular, thanks to that spectacular idea from Corey Long." Mr. Everett paused to let the audience clap for Corey. Trevor rolled his eyes.

"But we still don't know the cause of the smell. As seventh grade class president, what would you do to help? Cindy, you will go first."

Cindy lifted her chin high, feeling certain her answer was going to impress everyone. Because even though Libby had a new poster and her shoulders were confidently pulled back for some reason, Cindy planned to intimidate her with this answer for sure. Trevor she wasn't so worried about, because he was drying his sweaty palms on his jeans, so clearly he was already intimidated.

"Okay, so first? We keep dunking those hazmat guys because that's probably fun for them. And for seconds? We should run a scanning machine like the ones they have at airports and library checkouts to scan the school for foreign smelly objects, and if that doesn't work, we can get a dog that sniffs things and then we can *keep* the dog and make it our mascot! We'll put a pink bandanna on him—but hopefully it's a her—and we'll have a contest to name her, but I hope we call her Dixie. We can put funny sunglasses on Dixie, and we'll start a Web site where we post pictures of her in different bandannas, and we'll call the Web site aintdixiecute.com. I've already reserved the domain name! That's the awesomest thing, right? Vote for me!"

She bounced on her toes, certain that she had rocked that answer. There was no way Libby or Trevor would come up with a better suggestion.

"Trevor, you're next," Mr. Everett said.

Immediately, beads of sweat formed on Trevor's forehead. He couldn't believe how much sweat he had produced that week. This was getting ridiculous. Especially since he was now faced with yet another difficult sweat-inducing moment. The teacher had asked what they would do to help find the cause of the smell, and he was cursed with a need to answer questions correctly.

Trevor wanted so badly to just spill the truth. The words "My tuna sandwich caused the smell" were on the tip of his tongue. But he'd told Libby she could tell the audience the truth, since it was the best way for her to win this debate.

But then again, there was Mr. Everett . . . waiting for an answer. Trevor opened his mouth and started to form the words—but that's when he saw her.

Molly. She was out in the audience waving to get his attention. She was mouthing something to him: *Be cool.*

"Uh . . ." He stalled for a moment, trying to figure out why Molly was giving him advice. Especially advice he didn't know how to implement.

Mr. Everett tapped his watch. "You're almost out of time."

Between the beads of sweat on his forehead, Molly's advice, and Mr. Everett's watch, Trevor couldn't think of anything to say except one word: "Topeka?"

"That doesn't make sense, Trevor."

He dropped his head. "I'm sorry, sir." The gymnasium filled with laughter. At least he was on his way to losing the election like he'd planned.

Mr. Everett decided not to comment any further and moved on. "Libby, you're up."

Trevor braced himself. This had seemed like a good idea early this morning, but now, her telling everyone he was to blame for the smell made him want to disappear. Forever, preferably.

Libby paused dramatically before speaking. "I don't have a suggestion for helping the hazmat crew find the smell . . . because I know what *caused* the smell!"

Trevor looked away—he couldn't bear to watch

everyone's reaction. Their sneers. The taunting. All the ridicule—the thought of it was too much.

The audience filled with whispers and rumblings, but Libby quieted them all when she called out, "Wilson, come on up here, please!"

Trevor twisted his head around, wondering what was going on. Wilson? He wasn't part of the plan.

There were a couple of shrieks from students as they watched Wilson make his way down the aisle and up onto the stage carrying a wiggling burlap sack. He grabbed the microphone from Mr. Everett and announced, "Kids, no need to be alarmed. But I have found the source of the smell." He lifted the bag and wiggled it even more for added effect. "This here's a rabid long-tailed bush rat from Madagascar, a real sick one. Truly disgusting. To be honest, I'm not even sure which end the smell is coming from—"

But that was as far as Wilson could get into his explanation.

Cindy Applegate

Tapping foot,
waiting for the
debate to start
back up again

2:35 p.m.

So while we were waiting for that nice man in the space suit to come to, I went over to Marty and asked him for his advice on the second debate question. I know Marty and I aren't going out anymore, but he's the smartest guy I know, and I need his help.

It's not that I don't think I'll win. It's just . . . well, what Libby just pulled was a little surprising, and getting extra advice is always a good idea.

I'm not sure I can use EVERYTHING he suggested. I mean, he started talking really fast about focus groups and animal rights and making people feel intelligent, and I sort of got dizzy.

But just in case, I also have a backup plan. My surefire-can't-lose plan.

I can't lose.

Marty Nelson

Leaning against the
back wall, waiting
for the debate to
start up again

2:40 p.m.

Sure, I'll help Cindy out with her debate question. She seemed to really need some good advice. Plus, I'm not one to hold on to resentments. Plus, she's cute—yeah, I said it.

All she has to do is follow my advice exactly and she CAN'T LOSE. Which means she'll be in a good mood and then maybe I'll call her later tonight. I've got a good feeling about all this— the debate, and then my phone call.

Molly Decker

In the back
of the gym

2:41 p.m.

Yeah, I told Trevor to "be cool" while he was up there, because I didn't want him to go and ruin his reputation. He's had a pretty rough week and I didn't want to see him get laughed at. Plus, he hasn't spoken to me since the big argument between him and Libby, and I thought this would make him see I still want us to talk.

I feel bad about causing such a huge rift between those two. Maybe if I'd kept my mouth shut, none of this craziness would be happening right now.

And I guess . . . I miss him—he's my only real friend.

CHAPTER TWENTY-THREE

DWAYNE, THE HAZMAT GUY WHO HAD PASSED OUT, WAS given some smelling salts and taken down to the nurse's office to recuperate. Word was that he got light-headed around any animal that foamed at the mouth. Luckily, he started to feel much better when Wilson promised him that the rat had been "taken care of." (Which meant he'd thrown the sandwich away in the Dumpster out back.)

After a ten-minute break, the debate started again. "For the second and final question today"—Mr. Everett sounded a little tired at this point—"why do you want to be class president?"

Finally! Trevor thought. A standard student council debate question. Just like the ones he had rehearsed over and over at home.

But wait.

He *couldn't* answer this just like he had rehearsed at home—he needed to throw the debate. Except the thought of flubbing this question intentionally made his stomach twist into a knot.

But then it hit him how he could answer correctly *and* lose all at the same time. Trevor raised his hand. "Mr. Everett? Could I answer first?"

Mr. Everett shrugged. "I don't see why not. Go ahead, Trevor."

Trevor cleared his throat. "The truth is, I *don't* want to be class president. It's a job that takes a person who is organized and a planner and can get people involved in helping the school." He glanced over at Libby and smiled. "Those are all qualities I don't have. But there is someone on this stage who does. And I'm sure you'll find the right person to vote for, Westside."

Libby returned the smile while Cindy shook her head and looked the other way. Trevor heard some claps from the audience. It hit him how lucky he was to have a friend who would risk losing the election by asking Wilson to get everyone off his case about whether he caused the smell. Now his reputation wouldn't be obliterated, *and* Libby was about to win the debate. She had that multitasking thing down to a science.

"I want to go next!" Cindy said loudly. "Since you let Trevor choose to go first, I want to go now. Okay?"

She had a point. Mr. Everett nodded. "Go ahead, Miss Applegate. And just use your regular voice. Not too loud, not too soft." Even though his headache hoped for soft.

Cindy tossed her hair over her shoulder and got ready to answer. She looked out at Marty in the audience, who was mouthing words to her. "Let's see; I believe in equality for all students and equality for all animals, especially animals whose rights to fly freely without being hit by the carpool lane have been taken away. Like blue jays?" Cindy squinted as she looked at Marty, not able to read his lips, and unsure what to say next.

She gave up and turned away from him, grinning at the audience. "So here's the thing. I want to be student class president because you get to stand behind podiums. And I like standing behind podiums because I get to stand on a step stool, and they make me, like, a foot and a half taller. It is *seriously* wicked awesome up here."

She looked out into the faces of the audience members: they were blank. No response. Not even some sweet, supportive claps from Team Cindy! She knew there was only one thing left she could do in order to win this—

it was time to pull out her surefire-no-way-she-could-lose trick.

Because even though all this time she had been acting as if she knew she'd win, deep down, she was worried she wouldn't. Libby simply had too many things going for her—even though she didn't always seem to know it. So Cindy pulled out her one final trick, the one that would win her this election for sure.

"One more thing, Westside," she said. "As you know from my campaign materials, I'm running on a platform that we should bring back recess. However, I believe recess should not be people running around chaotically. No, I believe recess should be ten minutes of uninterrupted gum chewing. Because research says it increases your attention span *and* your happiness bars on a bar graph by *a lot*! So guess what, Westside Middle School?" She grinned even wider. Some say wider than they'd *ever* seen. "Free Hubba Bubba Strawberry Watermelon for everyone!!"

Cindy reached into a bowl she'd hidden behind the podium and flung handfuls of gum out to everyone in the audience. They jumped and cheered and whooped and hollered, and, in general, went completely bonkers. They chanted, "Cindy! Cindy! Cindy!"

This is bad . . . very bad, Trevor thought. There was no

way Libby could compete with the power of free gum. Especially not strawberry watermelon—that was just downright tasty.

Libby stepped back and took a deep breath. She could respect Cindy for coming up with that idea—it was an awesome move on her part. Tricky and tactless, but still awesome. And though she couldn't help but admit she was, in fact, a little intimidated, she was still in this race. Libby Gardner wasn't giving up.

Mr. Everett pulled out a bottled water and quickly popped two Excedrin. "Quiet down, students. We're not done yet. Libby, it's your turn."

Libby gripped the sides of her podium, taking a moment to figure out what to say next. What could she say to impress everyone after what Cindy just did? She stood frozen in the gleaming spotlight in awkward silence.

But she turned to get a glimpse of Trevor on the opposite side of the stage. He didn't say anything, just eyebrowed a quick message—left then right with a twitch at the end: *You can do this.*

Libby thought of everything he'd done for her—throwing away Jessica's note, saving her poster, being her manager year after year. She didn't want to let him down. Or her mom. Or her baby onesie.

Or herself.

She turned back to face the audience straight on. She couldn't win by giving away free gum, so she'd have to go with her own strengths. If there was anything Libby Gardner knew how to do, it was plan the details.

"Why do I want to be class president? Because I want to make things better for us around here," she announced loudly. "First things first . . . new dodgeballs. Better water pressure in the hallway fountains. Softer paper towels in the bathrooms. And one extra minute between passing periods."

There were a few supportive claps from the audience. That's when she added her last bit of event planning. "But most important, I will ask for another fall dance. Our last one got a little ruined by an unfortunate orange soda incident, so I propose we have a do-over."

Most of the audience clapped for this suggestion. There were even a couple of whistles. So Libby decided to pretty much . . . go for it. "And to help raise money for another dance?" She paused for dramatic effect. "We'll bring back one of those hazmat guys and put him in the dunk tank!"

The crowd clapped wildly. Libby welled up inside as she listened to her middle school classmates cheer for her. Not for gum. Not for glitter. Not for poof.

For her ideas.

Trevor smiled big—some say it was his biggest smile ever—and gave Libby a thumbs-up. Then he slyly reached down, grabbed a piece of strawberry watermelon gum off the floor, and stashed it in his pocket for later.

Marty Nelson

In the back of the gym, pacing—extreme

2:25 p.m.

Cindy went off-script. OFF-SCRIPT!! I gave her my expert advice and she THREW GUM? I mean, everyone likes free stuff, so it wasn't such a bad idea. But not DURING a debate. And yes, she's cute, but she's never going to win if she doesn't listen to other people's ideas.

So forget it. I quit. This campaign management stuff is taking up too much of my time anyway.

Besides, now I'll finally have a chance to watch my show tonight: *Extreme Catfish Hoarders*— the international one . . . It's WAY better.

But I'll probably still call Cindy tonight. No sense in giving up.

CHAPTER TWENTY-FOUR

AS EVERYONE FILED OUT OF THE GYM, THEY DROPPED their votes into a box and headed back to their last class of the day.

With only a couple of minutes remaining before the dismissal bell, the students waited for Vice Principal Decker to tally the votes and announce the winner. Trevor, Libby, and Cindy were all seated in Language Arts, anxiously awaiting the results.

There was one minute left until dismissal.

Then thirty seconds.

Then ten.

Vice Principal Decker planned to follow the suggestion in his leadership handbook and wait until the last possible moment to make the announcement; it

268

would shorten the amount of crying time.

At five seconds before dismissal, the intercom crackled. "Students, the votes have been tallied."

Trevor, Libby, and Cindy flicked looks between each other—a triangular glare down.

"The winner for seventh grade student class president is Libby Gardner!" *Ring.* "And you're dismissed."

Libby jumped up out of her desk, a huge smile on her face. She hurried over to Cindy and said, "Good job. Fun race this year."

Cindy hesitated, looking her over, then finally responded, "You did a good job, too. I can't wait to see how you do with your first project as president."

Before Libby could answer, she was quickly surrounded by her classmates, who were cheering and congratulating her. Trevor tried to get over to her, but there were too many people. The students funneled out of the room, pulling Libby through the door in a celebratory mob.

"Trevor! Meet me at my locker!" Libby shouted happily just before her face disappeared around the corner.

Trevor gathered his things. For the first time all week, he felt *good*. Everything was right in the world.

As he walked into the hall, he could see that an even larger group of students had formed around

Libby's locker. He pushed his way through the frantic crowd, but just before he reached her, a hand clamped down on his shoulder. Trevor whirled around—it was Corey Long.

"You're lucky you didn't win," Corey snarled.

"I know."

"Then why were you running?"

"To help Libby win."

Corey squinted like this hurt his head. "You make *no* sense, dude."

Trevor doubted he'd ever make sense to Corey Long. *Ignore him* was all Trevor could think to do. He looked away and stared up at the exit sign above the double doors, just the way he had earlier that week in the cafeteria. He figured that eventually Corey would simply have to go away, if only out of sheer boredom.

And sure enough, he was right.

Corey huffed, then brushed past him without another word and disappeared into the crowd.

Molly had witnessed the exchange between Trevor and Corey, and she raced over to Trevor, tapping his shoulder. "Trevor, you shouldn't let him get away."

"What do you mean? That went pretty well—I'm still in one piece, not mangled. Can't we mark this a win and go home?"

She folded her arms tightly. "Trevor, that guy is the reason you lost your popularity in the first place. He admitted it to me, that day you were wearing the hairnet. Corey turned the nozzle on your deodorant while you were hiding in the bathroom. And he shook up your soda at lunch when you were looking the other way."

"He what?!" Trevor yelped like a pitchy Chihuahua.

Molly poked him right in the middle of his chest. "Stand up to that guy. Stop looking away, stop hiding. Face him head-on." Then she nudged him with her elbow toward Corey, who was already down the hall and headed right toward Libby.

Trevor glanced back at Molly, and noted her bright blue eyes—the same ones that had convinced him that being cool meant doing what you wanted to do and not caring what other people thought. And then he remembered how she had mouthed the words "be cool" to him during the debate.

It was like she cared about his reputation. It was like she had his back.

Trevor decided if Molly believed he could actually face Corey, it was time to prove that he could.

Without hesitation, he took off and ran up to Corey before he could reach Libby. "You! You were the one who messed with my can of deodorant. And you shook up my bottle of soda at lunch." People noticed that Trevor had raised his voice—they couldn't believe what he was saying. Even *he* couldn't believe what he was saying.

Corey stepped back and faked that he knew nothing about it. "Huh? Me? Naw. No way."

Trevor considered yelling, being a jerk back to him. But

then he decided to go in a different direction. "You know, it's funny, Corey, how much time and effort you put into *my* day—all that planning and following me around. It must take a lot of work." He stuffed his hands into his pockets, all smooth-like, and smirked at Corey. The kids around them started to laugh, and Corey's face turned bright red.

"No, that's not . . . I just—"

"You must not have much going on in your own life. I'm sorry you're so bored, Corey." And before he could respond, Trevor calmly pushed past him, walked through the crowd, and went out the double doors right under the red exit sign without giving it a single glance. (He'd just meet up with Libby on the bus; a dramatic exit at this point was totally essential!)

It was clear his run-ins with Corey were far from over. But for today—in that moment—facing him head-on had felt great.

Libby found Trevor waiting to get on the bus. "There you are!" she said, joining him in line.

He smiled. "I told you you'd win."

"I definitely had to think on my toes, that's for sure."

"Bringing back the hazmat dunk tank? Nice touch. Everyone loved that!"

Libby winced. "Uh, yeah. About that? I sort of just flung that out there like Cindy did with that gum." She flopped her head in her hands. "How am I ever going to get them to agree to come back here? Especially now that they think our school is infested with rabid long-tailed bush rats."

Trevor realized he would have to tell the truth, at least to the hazmat crew. They were probably the only ones who would be happy to find out the smell was actually coming from his week-old tuna sandwich. "Put me in charge. I'll convince them to come back."

Libby patted him on the back. "Sure thing, Commander."

"That's Master Trevor, thank you very much."

They both laughed and stepped forward as the line moved ahead. But just before they got on the bus, they heard the crying.

Cindy Applegate

Carrying around
the step stool

3:01 p.m.

Not ME. I wasn't the one who was crying—come on, I'm not some sad sap. It was all the girls in my campaign crew, which was really sweet for them to get together in a huddle in the shape of a heart and cry SO HARD like that.

But mostly? I just think they're upset we aren't going to keep making T-shirts. It's so sad . . . I get it, really.

But we'd run out of cute T-shirt colors anyway, so it's not like we had a choice.

Am I upset I lost? Well, sure! But I don't DWELL on the negative—it gives me a slight head-ache.

And also? Libby will totally listen to all my suggestions, so I'm going to get my way no matter WHAT, so . . . win-win for me!

Hey, that sentence would look great on a T-shirt! Darn, I'm out of cute colors.

Molly Decker

Outside Vice
Principal Decker's
office, waiting for
her ride home

3:02 p.m.

So when everyone was crowded around Libby in the hall, I went up to her and asked if I could be in charge of snacks at the dance. I pretty much owe it to her for being a sorta cruddy campaign manager. And, to be honest, I also felt bad for ruining the dance the last time around. So yeah . . . the rumor is true . . . I apologized to her. Nicely, too.

Libby's response was classic—her eyes got all twitchy, and she started doing that twirl/chew thing with her hair, but I promised her THIS time I'd actually bring carrots or celery or whatever else from someone's yard she wanted. So now we're partners, I guess you'd say.

[deep, loud sigh]

We should have compromised. I mean, they DO make black glitter, so I suppose for the next class election we could get supercute buttons that poof black glitter in Cindy's face. I would not mind that one BIT.

WESTSIDE
MIDDLE SCHOOL

TWO WEEKS
LATER

CHAPTER TWENTY-FIVE

"**H**OLD STILL."

"Is duct tape really going to keep this together?" Trevor asked.

"I plan events all the time," Libby said. "When things go wrong, use duct tape."

Things had gone wrong . . . *very* wrong.

Trevor had placed five calls and had even made an impromptu drop-by visit to the town's Center for Disease Prevention to ask if someone in a hazmat suit would volunteer to be in their dunk tank at the school dance.

"It will raise money for the school! We need new dodgeballs and—" he had explained to the receptionist at the center, trying to convince him that this was for a worthy cause. But the receptionist had rolled his eyes and had sent Trevor on his way.

On Trevor's fifth call, the receptionist had transferred him to an actual manager, who not-so-politely told him that they would *not* attend the event at Westside due to a "clash of personalities" with a janitor by the name of Wilson.

Libby had taken the bad news fairly well—she didn't resort to organizing and reorganizing the Jones's *National Geographic* collection. Though she did snack on some ranch salad dressing while trying to hatch up an alternative plan.

She didn't want to let the students of Westside down, especially since this was her first "official" event as their newly elected president.

Now that she had no hazmat guy to dunk, she had to come up with the next best thing. And it didn't take long: Dress up Trevor in a homemade hazmat suit and just hope *real hard* that the duct tape would keep it sealed together.

"Maybe use two layers of the tape?" Trevor offered.

"Two layers. Good idea."

She finished his suit and said, "Now, I realize people may be disappointed that it's just you in a suit made out of pizza-box cardboard and duct tape. So you might get a little bored sitting there all alone. Sorry, Trev."

"Promise to at least bring me some snacks?"

"Promise."

Trevor took a deep breath. "And we're not taking dates this time, right?"

She smiled. "Not this time. This one's just for fun."

After they set Trevor up in the dunk tank, it didn't take long for them to see that Libby was clearly wrong. Trevor *wasn't* bored sitting at the dunk tank all alone.

When the students saw him in his homemade suit, they laughed—the good kind of laugh, not the bad kind. And suddenly, out of nowhere, some kids started nodding at him, a few gave him a thumbs-up, and Jake Jacobs even gave him a high five. It wasn't a fist bump, but it was a start. And they couldn't *wait* to get in line to dunk Trevor Jones.

After a successful night of dancing and dunking, Trevor

and Libby sat on the bleachers taking in the scene, glad they had finally pulled together an amazing fall dance.

But before Trevor could congratulate her, Corey walked up to them. This made Trevor nervous; his palms immediately did that clammy thing.

"I threw away all the cups and plates," Corey said to Libby.

"Silverware, too?"

"Yep."

"And the chairs?"

"Stacked them five high, just like you asked."

Trevor wondered, What in the parallel universe is going on?!

"Thanks, Corey."

"No problem."

He smiled at her. She smiled at him.

Trevor almost fell off of his bleacher.

When Corey was gone, Trevor blurted out, "What was that? Did I just dream that or was it for real?"

Libby laughed. "It was for real. Corey came to me earlier and said he felt bad about asking me to the last dance for algebra answers and he wanted to make it up to me. So I put him on cleanup duty. It's a win-win, right?"

"Sure, I guess. Except he's now sweeping the floors. Which is weird. Because he's Corey Long and all."

Libby looked over at Corey, who was happily sweeping, which he wasn't even asked to do. "Huh."

"He may be interested in being more than friends, Lib."

She blushed. "You think?"

"What do *you* think?"

Libby straightened her skirt and said, "We're just friends. But it's probably something that needs some further research."

"How'd I know you'd say that?"

She hopped up from the bleachers and pulled a quarter from her pocket. "Hey, I haven't had a turn yet. Let me dunk you?"

Trevor shuffled toward the tank, shreds of duct tape scraping along the floor. "Of course, Lib. That's what friends are for."

I suggest checking the teacher's lounge. According to page ninety-three of Boys' Life, bad smells can come from refrigerators that have not been cleaned out and rumor has it that teachers are busy.

The other possibility is an old roast beef sandwich in my locker. I lost it there a while ago and haven't seen it since. Sorry about that. If you find it, please return it to me unharmed, no questions asked.

~~Marty~~
Anonymous

ROBIN MELLOM used to teach middle schoolers and now she writes about them. (Any resemblance between fictional characters and her previous real-life students is purely coincidental. Probably.) She is also the author of *The Classroom: The Epic Documentary of a Not-Yet Epic Kid* and *Ditched: A Love Story*. She lives with her husband and son on the Central Coast of California.

Visit www.robinmellom.com for exclusive CLASSROOM content!

- Documentary outtakes!
- Inside sneak peeks!
- News on upcoming books!
- Answers to your questions!

(And don't forget to follow Robin on Twitter @robinmellom.)

Through a freak incident involving a school bus, a Labrador retriever, and twenty-four rolls of toilet paper, **STEPHEN GILPIN** knew that someday he would be an artist. He applied himself diligently, and many years later he has found himself the illustrator of around thirty children's books. He lives in Hiawatha, Kansas, with his genius wife, Angie, and a whole bunch of kids. Visit his Web site at www.sgilpin.com.